Praise for *Out of Dark Places*

A 'has been' musical genius with a propensity for numbing his highly sensitive and tortured psyche in a bottle of Scotch, Lukas, main character in *Out of Dark Places*, is imprisoned in limbo between the surreal world of his vivid and anguishing visions and the world of reality, compassion and second chances that secondary main character, Katie, beckons him, out of love, to return to.

Author Jeff Gephart develops his characters with multi-layered complexities and fascinations with the kind of sterling finesse rarely found …. We are invited into and captivated within the moody, macabre realms of Lukas's mind's eye. *Out of Dark Places* takes us on a multi-dimensional, other-worldly trip told mostly in first person present tense, but often jumping back and forth through time—adding to the non-linear, bewildered sense of disorientation Lukas lives, drinks, and struggles his way through.

The author spins a tale that builds inexorably in tension and mounting passion. The question at the end comes down to this: can a washed up, lonely, afraid, bitter, drunken and delusional, formerly great pianist do the right thing in a world he feels is fundamentally faulted—all wrong—and, will he be able to 'see' the love that binds and brings him back—in the form of Katie … before it's too late to stop the tragedy he has wilfully set in motion?

~ **Marvin D Wilson**, author of *Beware the Devil's Hug, Owen Fiddler,* and *I Romanced the Stone (Memoirs of a Recovering Hippie)*

The author's fascination with the human psyche is both clinical and artistic. His protagonist Lukas examines every casual one-time passer-by with an eye of a painter or a prophet, finding messages and clues in every detail. His painful sensitivity and heightened intuition cause him a great deal of unease. The narrative is written in the present tense, and the progression of the plot is not always linear, which contributes to the feeling of being out of time. The novel is set in a different dimension. It's marked by the exquisite, subtle moodiness of 1970s French films.

~**Marina Julia Neary**, author of *Brendan Malone: the Last Fenian*

Out of Dark Places

Jeff Gephart

Prologue

"Jingle singers are the worst," Nora said. "The lowest of the low. By far the most disconsolate people on earth." She said it matter-of-factly, in the same detached tone with which she said most things, the weary, didactic manner of someone who already has everything figured out, yet finds explaining any of it to be tedious.

Miles glanced at her, over the top of his glasses, then continued rolling his cigarette. He said nothing. He didn't have to ask. To him, Nora seemed to talk like only people on TV talked. Her random statements were obviously introductory, crafted to induce curiosity, but Miles had gotten past the habit of asking her to explain. She would soon clarify, without prodding. She always did.

"Garbagemen—wait, trash collectors," Nora continued, seemingly content to let Miles' silence serve as substitute for the obligatory request for elaboration for which she had been hoping. "I hate to call them garbagemen; it's such an ugly compound word. But my point is, trash collectors have it rough." She paused, only for a moment, as if allowing Miles a chance to disagree. He didn't. She resumed.

"However, I would imagine that plenty of men choose that particular occupation, simply for the salary. Or perhaps they prefer the early morning work hours. Or maybe, just the mere lack of ambiguity involved with the task itself."

Miles blotted his tongue along the frail edge of the rolling paper and squeezed the gnarled cigarette into shape. "What about people that work at a 7-11 or something?" he asked, without looking up. Sometimes he enjoyed playing along, contributing something to her diatribe just to prove he had been listening, once she had assumed he wasn't.

She didn't miss a beat. "The late hours, obviously. Night owls. Again, a conscious choice." She watched him light his cigarette, her eyes never meeting his. "You're only proving my point."

Miles reached around the cash register and flipped a switch. The green neon Heineken sign in the main window and its many reflections in the room's mirrors blinked out of sight. Miles leaned forward against the bar, face to face with Nora. "And what exactly was your point, again," he asked, with a grin.

Nora swirled the last remnants of the martini in her glass and watched the whirlpool. "My point, is that many of the jobs that our society deems as pathetic, dead-end jobs really aren't, because they have been deliberately chosen by their ... by the ... well, by the people that do those jobs."

Miles tried to conceal a smirk. He found himself entertained by Nora, always had been. Even now, when her looks were starting to abandon her, Miles still considered her enormously engaging. That's probably why he hadn't charged her for a drink in over two years. Yeah, she was a total caricature—her melodramatic mannerisms, her awkwardly sophisticated diction. But in her own way, she was genuine. She believed whole-heartedly in herself, with the earnest conviction of someone who had long ago forgotten the difference between real behavior and the mimicking of it. Most nights, after her last set, Nora would linger at the bar, nursing a drink, and keep Miles company as he closed up for the night. Her speech was peppered with academic words, delivered with a detached, philosophical tone that didn't seem to fit with the rather extreme commonness of her appearance. She talked about the banality of life. Miles didn't know what banality meant, exactly. He didn't know the definitions of a lot of the words she used. He did know the meaning of the word 'pretentious', however. In over two decades of running a nightclub in a city like this one, Lord knows he had encountered more than his share of pretension. But the label didn't seem to fit Nora, the better he got to know her. His perception of her had changed since he'd hired her. He viewed her with a mixture of amusement and pity, yet in some small way that he wasn't able to define, he wished he were more like her.

"But let me tell you something, Miles." Nora gulped down the last of her martini and pointed at him, like she was admonishing a child. "Nobody—I mean nobody—chooses to be a jingle singer." She shook her head slowly for dramatic emphasis. "When you're listening to the radio, and you hear some poor woman singing her little heart out about a discount mattress store, or how Gillette is the best a man can get, it should make you absolutely want to weep. Because every one of those singers—every voice you hear on every commercial—they all had big dreams when they started out. You know? They wanted to be Billie Holiday, or John Lennon. They wanted to matter. They didn't want to be some faceless voice, singing some cheery drivel about fast food, or car insurance. They didn't choose that! It's what they got stuck with."

Nora swiveled on her stool, casting a longing gaze out the window into the city's stillness, as if trying to recreate a pose she'd seen an actor take once in a movie. "Everybody who records a jingle for some lousy company—it's because they never became what they always hoped they would be." She sighed. "Jingle singers are the voices of broken dreams. And that's what makes them the most disconsolate people on earth."

Miles nodded, the way he always nodded, waiting to see if her soliloquy had run its course. Then he smiled at her, not needing to fake the fondness he felt. "You gonna be alright getting home?"

She nodded, without looking at him. Then, as if snapping out of a trance, she shot him a wry look, out from under heavy eyelids. "I'll be fine," she said. She stood, and began a slow and ungraceful gait toward the exit.

"Same time tomorrow, hey?" Miles called.

She turned back toward him, smiling without satisfaction. "What else?" she shrugged.

***

Upon confronting the rude chill of Chicago's early morning, Nora decided to walk home, just to spite the uncivil weather. It was a dreary trek.

Nearly twenty minutes later, when she at last began to climb the steps of her apartment building, her legs were rubbery, and the night's darkness had begun to give way to the grayness of a new day.

Entering her apartment, Nora squinted at the harsh light cast by the chandelier above the dining room table. Her mother and her daughter were seated at the table eating cold cereal, and both turned toward her.

"Hi Mommy!" Katie chirped.

"Hey, pumpkin."

Her mother held a steaming cup of coffee in both hands and gently blew into it. "Good morning," she said, making the carefully pronounced words sound accusatory, in a fashion that she had perfected over the years.

Nora dropped her purse beside the doorway and began unbuttoning her bulky winter coat. It always discombobulated her when she came home ready for night and encountered her family preparing for a new day. She took a moment to let her eyes adjust to the brightness of the room.

"I told you she'd be here in time," her mother said softly to Katie. "Why don't you read her your essay, see what she thinks?"

The little girl snatched a wrinkled piece of notebook paper from the table beside her and wiggled out of her chair. Her grandmother rose and carefully cleared the table of their breakfast dishes. As Katie bounced over to her mother, Nora walked briskly past her to the kitchen. "Give me a minute, okay? It's been a long night for Mommy."

"No doubt," Grandmother said, following her into the kitchen. "The club closed over two hours ago. Where have you been?"

Nora leaned against the sink, her back to her mother, and sighed deeply. "I'd rather not hear about it right now, Mother."

Grandmother reached around her and placed the cereal bowls onto a stack of plates and pans already sitting in the sink from last night's dinner. "Would you like to take it to the other room?"

"No, Mother," Nora replied, curtly, and a bit too loud. "I don't want to talk about it in the other room, nor in this room. I've had a long night, and I just wish to be left alone so I can go to bed." Nora looked down at the pile of dirty dishes, closed her eyes, and let her shoulders sag with another exaggerated sigh.

"I would have taken care of the dishes for you," her mother said, "but my arthritis is acting up something terrible today. It was painful enough just to prepare a meal for your daughter."

Nora glared at her. "Don't," she said.

Grandmother turned and ushered Katie, who had been standing timidly in the doorway, out of the kitchen. "Katie, go on and brush your teeth, and then you can read Mommy your essay. The school bus will be here soon." The little girl disappeared down the hallway. Leaning against the kitchen doorway, the old woman crossed her arms across her chest and fixed her stare on Nora.

"Did you drive home in this condition?" she said without an interrogative tone. "You could hurt somebody, you know."

Still poring over the dishes in the sink, Nora grinned bitterly. "Everybody hurts, Mother. It's one of the conditions of being alive."

Unflinching, she said, "I want you to listen to your daughter's essay. She worked very hard on it."

Nora nodded. "Of course," she said, her tone cruel, "Right away. I can't think of anything more vital to the survival of society than a second grade essay." She paused. "Except for maybe these dishes," she continued, gesturing angrily toward the sink. "I guess I better take care of these first, to spare your aching joints."

Abruptly she bent down and flung open the cabinet door beneath the sink. She yanked a tall white trash can out onto the floor and began grabbing dirty dishes from the sink, two and three at a time, hurling them into the trash. When the sink was emptied, she replaced the trash can, kicked the cabinet shut, and spun to face her mother, seething.

"There. The dishes are all taken care of. We can all rest easy now!" She turned and snatched a glass that was drying upside down on the dish drainer and clanked it down on the countertop. Reaching for a vodka bottle from a shelf in a high cabinet, she poured herself half a glassful and left the opened bottle on the counter. She brushed past her mother into the living room, and then stopped in her tracks. Katie stood in the hallway facing her, clutching the piece of notebook paper in her hand.

"Do you wanna hear my essay now, Mommy?"

Nora drew a deep breath and let it out, slow, so tired. "Of course," she said, then turned and plopped down on the worn sofa. Holding the glass in her right hand against the sofa cushion, she massaged her forehead with her left, as Katie moved to stand in front of her rigidly, like a nervous candidate about to deliver a keynote speech.

"It's an essay for class. It's called 'My Hero.'"

"Just read it, pumpkin," Nora interjected impatiently, then lightened her tone. "Okay? Just read it to me."

The little girl's lips twitched, silently rehearsing the first few words, her forehead clenched in concentration. "My hero is my mommy," she began.

Nora closed her eyes, letting out another subdued sigh.

Katie continued, her eyes glued to the paper. She read slowly, precisely. "My mommy is the most beautiful lady in the world. She is a singer, and her voice is very pretty. She has brown hair. She is very tall. She has a lot of pretty dresses, and she wears earrings in her ears that are made of real diam—dime—diamonds …" She paused when she stumbled on the word, and swallowed hard. She risked a sheepish glance at her mother, fearful of a disappointed expression. Instead, she saw no expression at all. Nora was splayed on the couch, her head resting back against the wall, left hand dangling over the side of the sofa, right hand now perfectly still, lightly balancing the glass against the beige sofa cushion. Katie could tell from her steady, deep breathing that she had fallen asleep. She stared for a long moment, as if trying to decode a hidden picture puzzle, her eyes absorbing every detail of her mother's sleeping form. Then the little girl tentatively wrested the drink from Nora's slumbering grasp and placed it on the coffee table. She gazed with a blank, resigned expression upon the sleeping woman for just a moment longer, then crossed the room. Carefully folding her essay and sliding it inside her backpack, she quietly closed the zipper, slung the bag onto her back, and exited through the front door without a sound.

It would be exactly one year later to the day that Katie's unremarkable world would change forever.

Part One

Chapter One

It's 4:56 in the rain.

Any other day, any other kind of weather, and it's just a few minutes before five. Almost happy hour. But 4:56 in the rain is different. Nothing good happens in the rain.

Perhaps she's not coming, Lukas thinks. Staring through the thick windowpane as the rain cascades over it in billowy sheets is like watching the world from behind a waterfall. Not as magical, but just as isolating.

Lukas's eyes drift toward a particular patch of soggy grass close to the house in the backyard. The waterfall effect makes it difficult to judge distance, but Lukas knows the spot well. He wonders if archaeologists a few generations from now will dig up that spot and unearth tiny pieces of antiquated stereo components, put them on display in a museum somewhere, and marvel at the primitive way in which twentieth century humans lived their trifling lives.

Lukas Willow's footsteps, ordinarily loud against the ancient oak hardwood floor, have trouble competing against the nearby sound of water raging through the tin gutters as he makes his way across the unlit parlor. The furnishings are sparse. A coffee table with a deep brown finish centers the symmetrical layout of the room, and it matches the end tables on either side of a dilapidated maroon sofa. All three surfaces are barren, covered only by faint stains which have alternately darkened and lightened scores of small circles and half-circles onto the wooden surfaces. The room smells as quiet as it looks. Cold, like the rest of the house. Lukas sets a wet glass down on the left end table and creates another dark circle. He grabs the Glenfiddich and drains the last drops of liquid from the bottle into his glass. Placing the empty bottle gingerly into a wastebasket near his feet, he stoops to look for ice cubes in the adjacent mini freezer. This freezer should sit higher, on top of something, he thinks. Knees don't bend like they used to.

A sudden tapping rattles the glass part of the front door.

Lukas is undeterred by the interruption; his ice cubes are frozen together into one misshapen conglomeration. Scanning his dusty surroundings, he retrieves a brass letter opener from a nearby countertop and chips off a few chunks of ice.

Again the knocking, louder this time, urgent. He scoops the ice gently into his glass, making sure not to spill, and uses the letter opener to stir. Wearily, he straightens his legs and ambles toward the front door.

Katherine Reiker looks older than twenty-one. Her hair, when not soaked and matted to her head, is probably the same dark brown color as her upturned eyebrows. Her narrow, wiry shoulders are shivering. "Mister Willow?" she says, but Lukas has already turned and started walking back inside. She follows. "I'm Katie," she says, pausing just inside the door to shake off some of the excess wetness. "I'm sorry I'm so late."

Even drenched, she's pretty. It's so easy for twenty-one-year-old girls to be pretty. Late Katie. "I have a doorbell," Lukas says.

"I'm sorry." It sounds like she really is. Lukas feels a stab of uneasiness. That didn't come out right.

"I have somewhere to be, but you can take a quick look to get an idea of the place if you'd like," Lukas says, listening to the rain. This isn't the sort of rain that just happens to fall; it is hurtling toward the earth, determined, as if each drop has its own vital mission to accomplish upon landing. If nothing else, he likes the sound of serious rain; it goes well with Scotch.

"That'd be great," Katie says, and a lopsided smile stretches across her face that mutes the rain.

Lukas turns and crosses the stone-tiled floor of the alcove toward the staircase, passing by a two-level bookshelf built into the wall that displays only two identical rectangles of dust. Although the uneven wooden stairs look like relics, they register barely an audible creak as Katie follows him up. The clacking of her clogs against the rigid wood, however, is deafening. At the top of the stairs, Lukas pauses outside the door, motioning for Katie to go inside. The walk up the stairs has left him lightheaded. Too many drinks, possibly. Too few trips to this part of the house, probably. Not enough drinks … definitely.

The girl steps lightly into the old apartment-style room and looks around, as if silently assessing its livability. The doorframe is low, and Lukas would have to slouch his lanky frame to pass under it, but he stays just outside, on the landing. He has no interest in the old room; he knows it well. It hasn't changed much since he'd rented it as a student, long before he bought the house. Not much has been added. A few items have been removed. But everything has changed.

"I was excited to see your ad," Katie says, her slender fingers delicately examining a discolored pine desk in the corner. The room is a humble space, with a slanted ceiling and a lone window shrouded by a dusty film that suggests it hasn't been disturbed in years. Somber drips of water leak slowly from a tiny sink in one corner. A twin-sized bed, lumpy and thin, sits on cinderblock supports across from the desk, and has been covered by boxes and warped stacks of papers, bundled with roughly tied twine. Lukas had mentioned over the phone that he had been using the room primarily for storage, and had promised to clean it out, but he hadn't yet gotten around to it. Standing near the doorway,

Katie shrugs awkwardly, and Lukas has no idea how to interpret the gesture. She scans the room again, smiles, and says, "I wasn't sure I'd be able to find a place this close to the start of the semester."

"You got good and soaked out there," Lukas notes. He feels old. Particularly in a college town, particularly beside Katie. So young, soaked and she doesn't even care; she'll bounce back. "Umbrellas aren't as popular as they used to be, I s'pose."

"Actually, I have one, but I was running late and forgot it." Katie turns to meet his gaze, then quickly turns away. She stares pointedly at the old piano bench, inconspicuous upon first glance from its neglected spot beneath three boxes of yellowed paperback books. "Then I forgot to bring the address with me and went to the wrong house at first."

Forgetful Katie. Free-spirited, maybe. Still young enough to get away with it. She runs her fingers through the wet, shoulder-length strands of her hair, and paces around the room, scanning each direction as if looking for something in particular. "God, I must look ridiculous," she says with an unsure grin. Lukas catches himself on the verge of smiling. Somehow, her remark didn't sound as phony as it should have. Funny how a pretty girl's self-consciousness somehow makes her even prettier. She stops and faces him. "Aren't there any mirrors in this place?"

The question catches Lukas off guard. He gulps the last watered-down sip of Scotch and shakes his head. He doesn't need to run a mental inventory of the house's supplies. "No," is all he says.

Chapter Two

Approaching the age of fifty is a distasteful milestone. A man can no longer deny, nor can he feign ignorance of, the fact that he has aged, that his body does not function with the same competence and resiliency that it once did. He starts to fade, to become camouflaged to an entire generation that now only views him as part of a trivial human landscape of background scenery—one of the multitude of old people. No longer an individual. It makes some men despondent, betrayed by a feeling of uselessness. Others grow bitter, realizing that the world is still able to operate just fine without their input, leaving them feeling more unused than useless. For Lukas the problem is neither. His disappointment initiates from the fact that he is still needed, that he is in fact depended on, that his services are still required, when what he most longs for is to simply disappear.

Lukas eases his Volvo into the concrete driveway and shifts into park. The rain has almost dissipated now, but nearly ten hours of steady downpour have rendered the fractured concrete the color of riverbank mud, except for sporadic dandelions sprouting from cracks, and the scattered constellations of white spots that remain from when Lukas painted the garage door with unsteady hands a summer ago. Whenever rain darkens the driveway, the paint splotches show up more prominently, as if trying to remind Lukas of something that had tormented him at the time, something which now has run together into a muddled memory of vague discontent.

It is not exaggeration to say that Lukas gives no thought to his physical appearance. He shaves with a rough razor, sans shaving cream, while in the shower. His angular hairline has begun to retreat towards the back of his scalp, and the brown has now become frosted with patches of gray around the temples that make him appear more shopworn than distinguished. He had been a smoker only for a brief period during his youth, but years of drinking have begun to leave their trace on his countenance in the form of sagging features and premature wrinkles. His eyes, once vibrant and penetrating, have become sunken and dull gray, and they reflect the resigned stoicism of someone who has willfully eradicated his own passions.

Shutting off the engine of his trusty Volvo, he runs his hand through the still-brown part of his hair and squints curiously at the beige Ford Tempo parked beside him in front of the garage. He draws a deep breath, then another. He steps out of the car and walks slowly up to the porch, making no effort to avoid getting wet. He suspects he knows to whom the car belongs. Good things never happen when it rains. One more Scotch would've been a decent idea, he thinks.

The old front door drags sluggishly across the fluff of the new carpet as Lukas lets himself inside. In the kitchen, a blonde woman in a pressed white uniform is stuffing folders and notebooks into a large cloth handbag. She looks up at Lukas, who stands immobile. Thickly applied makeup does little to hide the tiny lines that crease her forehead and the areas around her eyes and mouth. Her pale blue eyes seem to cower at the sight of Lukas, yet the rest of her face does not so much as twitch. Her light brown hair is pulled back into a tight ponytail and reveals highlights of blonde and silver. She faces him.

"Hi Luke," she says in a half-whisper.

The rain intensifies, grows louder. Or does he simply imagine that it does? Lukas's face remains expressionless, as if he were gazing into an empty room. His suspicions about the car confirmed, he looks down at the dull tiles of the kitchen floor. "Susan," he mutters perfunctorily. Although outwardly he appears unaffected, her presence disconcerts him. In Lukas's mind he has transformed her from an actual human being into a mere symbol, an iconic reminder of a time he's tried to forget. Over the years Lukas has systematically severed contact with such people for the most part. But despite the carefully self-preserving architecture with which Lukas has constructed his present existence, there are occasional reminders that cruelly spring forth to reinforce to him that—in truth—life operates beyond his control. Susan is one such reminder. And if she is a whisper that cannot be fully ignored, then the reminder living on the floor directly above where they stand is a blast siren blaring from the mountaintops of the world.

Regaining his bearings, Lukas walks around to the far side of the kitchen table, opposite her. "Didn't expect to see you here," he says.

"You didn't?"

"No, I didn't." And Lukas turns to face her, his gray eyes unblinking.

"I thought your mother had told you," she says, dropping his gaze and gently placing the rest of her things in the bag. After a moment, she swallows and says, "I'm late for class. Why don't you go up and see her? She's resting."

Lukas says nothing. He begins to sort through the mail on the table, separating the important from the unimportant. Susan shoulders her bag, quietly picks up her keys, and leaves the house without looking back. Lukas continues to sort. Mail. Bills. Obligations.

***

His mother's room is over-decorated with framed photographs, more like a time capsule or museum exhibit than an area intended for living. The dim light cast from a hurricane lamp on the bedside nightstand makes the blueberry wallpaper look black and far away. The perpetual mechanical sigh of the portable vaporizer is the room's only audible narration. From her bed, the old woman's features wrinkle into a smile when she sees Lukas at the door.

"Come on in."

"How you feelin', Gladys?"

She shakes her head. "Like a million counterfeit bucks, kiddo."

Lukas pulls a chair to the bedside and sits. Nothing is said. The padding on the chair is shot; it should've been replaced years ago. The old woman picks up a cigarette from the nightstand and lights it with a shaky hand. "Susan wants me to quit," she says. "But at this stage of the game, I think the point is moot." Her voice is raspy, but with a hint of vitality that belies her frail appearance. "My goodness, you should've heard me coughing a minute ago. I sounded like you, when you were little." She looks up at the ceiling and exhales a faint column of smoke. "Remember how you used to have those coughing fits?" she says, an odd trace of a smile on her lips as she takes another drag.

"I found someone to rent the upstairs," Lukas says.

She pauses, not breathing in or out, looks at him. "A student?"

"Yeah, a girl. Music major."

The woman's thinning eyebrows rise. She expels more smoke. "It's a good room for aspiring musicians." Her smile gets no reaction from Lukas. "She's got a tough act to follow, though." She reaches for Lukas's hand, but he pulls it away.

"The point is, I'll be able to take care of the nurse. I'll call them tomorrow."

"Save your money. I don't need a nurse. Susan is going to look after me."

Lukas takes a moment to respond. He forces himself to focus on tangibles, to keep the bewilderment in check. White uniform. Drives a Ford Tempo. There are bills on the table downstairs. "How often," he asks, his tone even.

"Full time. She's going to be staying here."

Lukas stands and walks to the wall, silently studying a black and white photograph of a young couple in formalwear. His parents, before they were married, on a sunny day. Of course. No one takes pictures on rainy days.

"You never cared for Susan," the old woman says, "And I never quite understood why."

"It's not important." Not anymore. Maybe it was, once. His back turned toward his mother, Lukas draws a deep breath, then exhales forcefully, as if ridding himself of tainted air. It's not important. Nothing his mother needs to know about, at any rate. Some things are better left unknown. And if that's not possible, then forgotten about is the next best thing.

"She's your brother's widow. If you squint your eyes, that's almost like family."

"Doesn't she work during the day?" Lukas is caught up in the pictures, temporarily mesmerized by the evidence that his parents were once younger than he is now. It's the only photograph of his father that made it into a frame. He wasn't around for many photo shoots. String of bad weather, perhaps. Or bad luck, depending on whom you talk to.

"Only three days a week."

"And what's this class she's going to right now?"

"She's furthering her education at the hospital, two nights a week. I don't need a babysitter twenty-four hours a day." Lukas moves to the window, looks out at the brooding afternoon. The rain is back. Serious rain, of singular intent. He thinks of Katie, visualizes her walking up to the wrong house in the rain. Late Katie. He smiles. Stay late, Katie. As long as you can.

The room vaporizer maintains its whispery vigil. The old woman clears her throat. "Look, her landlord is selling the house. She has no place else to go. She needs me." She takes a careful drag from her cigarette and then adds, "And I need somebody."

Lukas doesn't like the tone of that last word. It's not a good day for talking. It never is. "Somebody besides me," he hears himself say.

"Somebody that's not afraid to give an old lady a hug once in a while."

Lukas turns to face her. He long ago mastered the ability to transform his face into a barren landscape, devoid of any trace of emotion.

The old woman turns away, jams out the butt of her cigarette. She can't face the expressionless face. "Look kiddo, I owe it to her, alright?" she mutters, a hint of exasperation creeping into her tone.

"How do you figure?"

"I owe it to Stephen. I figure if I can help out his widow, maybe it'll even up my account a little bit."

"You don't owe Stephen anything either."

"Of course I do," she says, struggling to cover herself with a wool blanket. "I committed the worst sin a mother ever can."

Lukas helps her tuck herself under the huge blanket. He notices her stringy, wobbling arms, flesh hanging sadly from bone. This is his mother, not the spirited girl in the photograph. "Which is?" he says quietly, feeling a twinge of premonition.

She manages a feeble smile. "I don't think I did a very good job of hiding the fact that I never loved him like I loved his brother."

It is the first time it has been said out loud. The admission would've produced shockwaves in most people, but the needle inside Lukas doesn't even fluctuate. His face remains blank as he turns toward the bedroom door. Time to go to work. Don't forget the mail on the kitchen table. Bills. Obligations.

Chapter Three

Data. That's what it all comes down to. Keeping careful records. Babysitting the ever-vacillating under-earth. Monitoring plate shifts. Mediating convergent and divergent boundary disputes. P Waves. S Waves. Hoping nothing is about to happen. Metal desk, metal file cabinets, broken office chair. All gray. This is the time of night Lukas usually spends indoors, in his undecorated office, compiling, analyzing, and filing the data he's collected during the day. Seismology. The study of hidden pressure, turbulence beneath a calm exterior. It's a job made necessary by all the oil drilling and coal mining in the area. Maybe not necessary; the larger and more delicate sensors at the State Observation Center would probably pick up anything much earlier than the twenty-five-year-old seismograph equipment in Lukas's office possibly could, but it makes the people of the town feel better to know there's an actual person in the little office, keeping an eye on things. Window-dressing at the most. But it's a job. And it's a one-man job. That's what Lukas likes about it.

The only color that has found its way into the tiny office is spread thickly on a stretched canvas, leaning against the wall from its perch atop the dented file cabinet. Lukas has never bothered to have it framed, let alone hang it up. A painting done by an old girlfriend from college. Julia Tannerly. Dark people on a beach, dancing ritualistically under a too-red sky. Lukas was never sure why he'd kept it. She had gone overboard with the reds. Sky was never that color, not anywhere he'd ever been anyway. But that was maybe why he liked it. At one time, they were going to find that place, Julia and him. That place with the deliriously red sky.

Lukas reaches for the bottom right drawer of his desk, but it sticks. It always sticks. When he yanks it open, he nearly topples a case of dirt samples. All for a nearly empty bottle of Scotch. Not even enough for a toast to Julia Tannerly. He wonders if she ever made it there. If maybe she waited on the beach under the red sky and looked around for him a while before she realized he wasn't coming. Did she wonder why not? Lukas replaces the bottle, too depressed to even throw it away, and closes the drawer.

It's too quiet in his office tonight, and it's never too quiet for Lukas. Time to go somewhere else. Someplace without noise, but not too quiet. Keep the pressure hidden.

***

Lukas turns to the next page and refolds his newspaper. He's not really reading—just bits and pieces mostly, but it looks like he's reading. It's enough of an appearance to avoid getting caught up in a conversation without seeming rude. Aloof he can handle, but he doesn't wish to seem ill mannered.

The Deer Pass Tavern is a hit-or-miss destination, depending on the night of the week and the clientele. Tonight, it suits Lukas just fine. By a stroke of luck, the wall speakers were fried by last night's thunderstorm; the only music emanates softly from a small radio beside the cash register. The bartender has propped it at an awkward angle so that the antenna cord could be strung precariously up the side of the cabinet. Even with the homemade modifications, the signal is weak, leaving the music pleasantly unobtrusive.

The bartender, a tall, broad man with shaggy, honey blond hair, looks as if he may have been some sort of athlete at one time. His face, weather-beaten with wrinkles that suggest an inordinate amount of time spent in the sun, creases easily in and out of a relaxed smile as he listens to the animated stories being told by a man wearing an oversized trucker's cap who is seated two stools down from Lukas. The man with the cap is exuberantly recounting a recent run-in he experienced with police officers for the bartender's—and clearly his own—amusement. He gestures exaggeratedly with his hands as he speaks, and he pauses now and then to suck thoughtfully on a cigarette, which Lukas guesses is merely a stall tactic to give him time to brainstorm more elaborate embellishments for his story.

Lukas tries to focus on the newspaper and his Scotch, but he keeps sneaking disdainful glances toward the bartender, who is openly engaged in transferring the remains of a nearly empty bottle of Jim Beam into an identical bottle that is about three quarters full. Combining the two in order to throw away one bottle, the way waitresses do with bottles of ketchup at greasy roadside diners. Lukas is appalled. Is nothing sacred?

As the clock behind the bar inches closer to ten o'clock, the only other patrons in the pub are a young man and woman seated at the short end of the bar, perpendicular to the man telling stories. They both sip at bottles of beer and seem to be listening half-heartedly to the other man's stories, occasionally grunting brief exchanges quietly with one another. An air of melancholy seems to hover around the couple the way cigarette smoke hangs in the air around the man with the trucker's cap, but Lukas determines to not think about it. He is glad for the resounding volume of the storyteller's voice, for his words are inane yet benign, and they make it impossible for Lukas to hear whatever small sadnesses pass between the young man and woman.

Lukas has drained the last of his Dewar's and set the empty glass to the inside edge of the bar in a silent signal that the bartender has yet to notice. He is about to call out for a refill, but he hesitates, nervous that anything he vocalizes will only call attention to him, and the bar's resident talker may construe it as an invitation to include him in the conversation. As he grapples momentarily with indecision, he is saved by the storyteller himself, whose boisterous request for another Bud Light spurs the bartender to look his way as well. Lukas nods, and the bartender fills a new glass and brings it to him. Lukas is mildly surprised that he didn't reuse the same glass, but smiles politely nonetheless.

"Hoo-ey!" the trucker declares, for no apparent reason other than the fact that he hasn't heard his own voice in several seconds.

Lukas takes a long sip from the ice-cold beverage. He smiles as he holds it in his mouth for a moment, and then he swallows. This one is noticeably stronger than the last. Perhaps the bartender has a touch of class to him after all. Lukas can feel a welcome sense of lightness beginning to seep back into his head.

The trucker gulps from his fresh Bud Light, then tips the bottle toward the bartender—as if about to impart some indispensable wisdom—as he continues his story. "So then the littler of the two gets right in my face and says, 'Do you want to go to jail, sir?'" The trucker is sneering, trying to imitate the sinister look the police officer had used on him. "Trying to intimidate me or something."

"That's how they do," the bartender says, smiling and shaking his head.

"Well, let me tell you something Johnny," the trucker continues, leaning closer. "I stayed right there in his face and I says to him, 'I been to jail, so if you're trying to scare me, you're gonna have to come up with something better than that.'"

Lukas no longer pretends not to be listening to the man's story. He watches the man talk, entertained by his over-the-top bravado tone, silently wondering how much of the story actually happened. Lukas is beginning to feel pleasantly mellow, the restrictive confines of his office becoming a distant memory. Mission accomplished.

The storyteller has taken another long sip from his bottle, and now nearly chokes on it as he tries to stifle a laugh. "I thought that little runt was gonna *piss his pants*. Hoo-ey! He backed right away from me then."

The bartender smiles. Lukas can't tell if it's a smile borne of politeness or whether he's as genuinely delighted as he seems. The young man and woman at the end of the bar exchange subdued grins.

The trucker is drunk on his own stardom. "Then he kind of lets his hand slide down his side, you know? To sort of rest near his holster, like he's about to start shooting or something." The trucker stands, imitating the policeman's pose. "Well, I knew that dude was more scared of me than I was of him, so I kinda take a step forward, you know? Just to mess with him. I says, 'And I been shot before, too, so I ain't scared of that neither.' Boy you shoulda seen the look on his face—like somebody just walked over his grave!" The trucker sits back down and slaps the bar in profound amusement. The girl at the end of the bar giggles.

The bartender stoops to retrieve an unopened bottle of tequila, then proceeds to cut away the plastic seal and remove the cap. He grabs a pourer spout from a supply he keeps in a Tupperware tub and gently squeezes it into place over the lip of the bottle. Now that it's ready for use, he places the bottle on an empty spot behind him on the service shelf. Lukas examines the rows of gleaming bottles for the tenth or twentieth time this evening, admiring the display. It's an impressive assortment for an establishment that most would call a dive bar. The tiered, leveled design of the shelves is for practical purposes, Lukas realizes, so bartenders can easily spot the particular bottle they're looking for. But the lustrous glass that covers each stepped shelf, the mirror installed as backdrop, the multi-angled lighting that makes each bottle of liquid appear luminescent and significant—all these perks have been added for the aesthetic pleasure of persons like himself. Those pilgrims who sometimes travel to bars simply to admire the grandeur of the display, to worship at the altar of alcohol. *And all the people said, 'Amen.'*

"Let me tell you something else, Johnny," the trucker starts up again. Lukas takes another swallow and swivels his stool to face the storyteller in a more head-on fashion, almost giddy that there is going to be more to the story. "Lots of guys claim to be tough, you know? Hell, that's why half the cops become cops in the first place, because they want to prove something. But everybody's afraid of something, whether they wanna admit it or not."

Lukas swivels his stool back to face the wall in front of him. The story is growing less entertaining and more philosophical. Lukas has no use for philosophy tonight.

The trucker continues, "Everybody's afraid of dying, right? Everybody. So when you come across a sonnovabitch who ain't afraid to die, I don't care who you are—you realize right quick just exactly how tough you really are." He stops to draw another careful drag from his cigarette. The ash extends almost an inch from the end of the lighted butt, and still it won't fall off. It looks more like the end of a stick of burning incense, the way the trucker keeps it balanced without dropping it. All around him on the bar are small piles of ash where his previous efforts have finally succumbed to gravity.

"Take this little squirt of a pig for example," he says, as the bartender opens a new bottle of vodka. "Probably thought he was a pretty tough guy, always able to make poor jerkoffs back down with a threat of jail or by wavin' his gun around. Them stupid mirror-looking sunglasses they all wear, supposed to make 'em look scary or something. Then he meets me, and he can tell I ain't a bit afraid of his scrawny little ass. He finds out he could pull out his nine and point it right in my face and I ain't even gonna flinch. Now he's scared, 'cause he realizes I ain't. Even guys who think they're hard get rattled when they run across somebody that can look death right in the eyeball and not even blink. Lots of people talk like they're that tough, but when you come across one who really is, believe me boy, you know it. And it's enough to scare anybody, even cops." The trucker looks over at the young couple at this point and nods, like Olivier taking a bow after the final act of *Hamlet*.

Lukas tips his glass back and drains the rest of the Scotch. He places the glass at the "refill spot" on the bar and smiles at the absurdity of it all. Over the years, Lukas has tried to learn to derive amusement from the same sorts of things that used to aggravate him. The trucker, for example. A rather obscene caricature sample of the hordes of deluded people that wander around their lives, lost in their idiocy. As a younger man, Lukas could only stomach so much of it. But now he has realized that such people are exactly where they need to be, doing what they need to do to get through the turbulent tragedy of life. Just doing what he does, in a different sort of way. And they're really harmless in most ways, after all, so why not enjoy what they bring to the table? Lukas could have lived without the trucker's musings on death and fear—these were subjects from which he sought distraction, not reminders. But the rest of the man's performance so far this evening has been painless, low brow entertainment. Like reality television, without the commercial interruptions.

The unsteady trucker manages to dismount his stool, announcing his intentions to "break the seal" in the men's room. Lukas almost acts on the impulse to applaud him on his way by, but decides against it and nods to the bartender for a refill.

Johnny obliges a moment later, sitting a fresh glass in front of Lukas and saying, "This one's on me, brother."

Lukas returns his smile with a grateful nod. A gentleman and a scholar. Perhaps he should frequent this place more often, he thinks. It's a nice change of pace from the sofa in his parlor. And better company.

With the trucker's absence, the scene grows quiet. The radio fades in and out, but the bartender doesn't seem to notice as he checks off inventory on a clipboard. Lukas allows his gaze to wander across the room and settle upon the young couple. They each stare at their own bottle of beer, expressionless.

23

"Wanna get a shot of SoCo?" the girl says suddenly. The young man doesn't respond. She resumes her glum staring at the bottle.

After a moment, the young man takes a sip of his beer and mutters, "Charlie said the same thing's happening at the plant in Morganville."

A silent alarm sounds in Lukas's head. He wishes the trucker would hurry up and return. He takes a liberal sip from his Dewar's and goes back to inspecting his newspaper. Suddenly an image of moving boxes and an over-packed old Mazda forms in his head. Lukas shakes his head and takes another sip, trying to force the vision from his consciousness.

"Please," he hears the girl say, "let's just have a drink and try to be happy."

Inwardly Lukas cringes at the preposterous statement. You can't try to be happy. You can try to be healthy, by eating right or exercising. You can take lessons and try to learn to play an instrument. But you can't try to be happy. It either happens or it doesn't.

Lukas feels an instantaneous and strong resentment towards the girl, as if his lighthearted mood was a balloon and she was brandishing a needle.

The bartender disappears into a back room, and Lukas is left alone with the downcast couple. He feels his throat tighten. He considers leaving cash on the bar and walking out. Then he hears the bathroom door swing open, and the trucker reappears. So does the bartender, carrying two new bottles of liquor. Lukas feels a slight resurgence of hope. He takes another sip.

"Hoo-ey, that's the good stuff right there," the trucker exclaims as he takes his seat. Lukas looks over. The bartender has begun opening a new bottle of Bacardi 151. Lukas is not a big fan of rum, but one had to appreciate any liquor with such a high percentage of alcohol content. For a second, Lukas considers ordering a round of shots for the bar. Maybe that would cheer the two cheerless young people at the end of the bar. Almost immediately he decides against it, realizing that such a gesture would surely result in his being dragged into a conversation. He decides to sit back and wait for the trucker to begin another soliloquy. The trucker sucks on another cigarette, greedily eyeing the bottle of 151. The bartender is struggling to fasten a pourer that appears to be too small to fit the mouth of the bottle.

Lukas determinedly avoids looking in the direction of the young couple, but it's no use. More images reveal themselves to him. Like a magnet he is being drawn closer to their shared pain. He has no control over it. His anathema. He lets his shoulders slouch.

The bartender is now pressing down with both hands, trying to force the pourer into position. All at once the force is too diagonal—not vertical enough—and the rum slams down sideways onto the bar. The lip of the bottle emits a deep brown stream that spills across the length of the bar before he can get it upright. The spilled liquor snakes its way to the spot where Lukas's own drink sits, and he watches it, mesmerized. Like a river choosing its own course across the terrain, it seems to be approaching him purposefully.

Barkeep curses. The trucker, after only a moment of stunned silence, lets out a hoot and declares, "Hoo-ey! That's about thirty bucks worth of profit you just sprinkled across the bar, Johnny!" He breaks into a raucous fit of laughter. The bartender produces a small rag, looks at the size of the spill he's created, and drops the rag, choosing instead to retrieve a new roll of paper towels from a cabinet beneath the bar. He glares at the trucker, which only increases the volume and force of the latter's laughter. His whole body is convulsing with uncontrollable shrieks and guffaws, and he is forced to set his Bud Light down to avoid spilling it.

The cigarette in his right hand sports another stump of ash, which is jarred free by the man's violent jocular spasms. As if in slow motion, the smoldering ash drops from the cigarette and lands in the spilled brown river. Immediately the rum ignites, producing a flame that rises several inches high and spreads down the length of the bar.

The immediacy of the flame's ignition causes both bartender and trucker to leap back in opposite directions away from the fire. The trucker falls backwards off his stool and lands in a clumsy heap on the stone floor. The couple, although safely out of the flame's reach, rise off their stools and watch in shock. The bartender stands hypnotized by the dancing tongues of the four-foot-long wall of fire.

The trucker clambers quickly back to his feet, his amusement now mixed with surprise and wonder. He gazes along the length of the blaze until his eyes lock onto Lukas's. His smile disappears. "Son of a bitch," he murmurs, the color draining from his face. The barkeep snaps out of his trance and looks toward Lukas.

Lukas, slumped upon his stool, stares transfixed at the yellowish translucent flame, as it dances only inches from his face and hands. He hasn't budged an inch.

Chapter Four

The next morning, for the third straight day, the sky is an uninterrupted expanse of gloomy gray. Instead of seeming like a sad, heavy shroud placed crudely over the earth, it gives Lukas the impression that this is in fact the sky's natural and eternal color, that the buoyant mask of brilliant blue it had occasionally employed before has been packed away forever.

At least it's not raining.

A cool breeze passes through him like the ebb of a tide. Lukas shuts his eyes and draws a deep breath through his nose. The air smells different up here, somehow, and there's more of a chill accompanying it. Perhaps the previous day's rain ushered in a cooler front, or perhaps it's the altitude. For an instant, Lukas feels dizzy; he reaches out his left hand to steady himself. The ancient brass surface of the bell is coarse, weather-beaten, and shockingly cool to the touch, causing Lukas's eyes to spring back open. He admires the silent grandeur of the antique bell, its sheer size. He could lean against it with his full weight if he chose, and still it wouldn't budge. He wonders how long it's been since it has been rung, and how such a task would actually be accomplished. Would two or three sturdy men have to work together to yank on a grizzled old rope, the way tower bells are rung in the old western movies? Lukas wonders if there's anyone left at the university who remembers what the bell sounds like. A recording of chimes was substituted for the authentic ringing of the bell more than a decade ago, but students during Lukas's tenure at the school had been privileged to hear the real thing. It seems perverse to Lukas that this very bell, which has come to symbolize the university the way the Eiffel Tower represents Paris—a stylized rendering of it adorns all official school documents as part of the logo— has only been seen, and not actually heard, by the past several generations of students who've attended the school. Lukas suspects that very few—if any—students have taken the opportunity to admire the bell from such an up close and intimate view as he now enjoys. Probably a few on a freshman dare, or during a late night drunken escapade, but as a rule students are not permitted access to the spot in the bell tower where Lukas now stands, mere inches from the grand old icon itself.

From this spot Lukas can view the entire campus at once, and most of the surrounding borough. Only the rolling peaks of the mountains to his right, and maybe a few of the oil derricks far to his left, claim greater elevation than the university's celebrated bell tower, perched atop Longkesh Music Hall. The sky above him appears two-dimensional, flat like a piece of sheet metal. The only depth he can sense is when he looks off into the distance or straight down into the courtyard. The pine trees sway slightly as breezes come and go, and from up here they look miniscule and feeble enough to be laid horizontal if a strong gale should push its way through. But other than that, the courtyard is appropriately quiescent. It is still too early for the college kids to be out and about, which is what Lukas had been hoping for. He has decided upon this location for its altitude and angle, not because he derives some twisted sense of gratification from the macabre. Holding onto the warped wooden frame of the tower, he leans out to peer down at the approximate spot where he'll land.

The courtyard is paved with red bricks, so after proper cleaning there should be no visible stains left to haunt future passersby. Lukas feels a prick of guilt and empathy for whomever will discover him today, though. And in a small school like this, everyone will soon hear about it, if not have the chance to see the gruesome display for themselves. Lukas has made peace with this reality, however, hoping that in some way his fate will serve as a cautionary tale to this next generation. That even though they won't know the specifics of his story, they will understand that his was a life that veered too far in the wrong direction until its course became irrevocable. And just possibly the memory of this tragic morning will be enough to subconsciously inspire them to pay more heed to their own actions than they otherwise would.

Another crisp breeze slingshots up from the quad below, forcing Lukas to once again grab hold of the splintered frame to steady himself. Out of the corner of his eye, Lukas thinks he sees the huge bell sway, but when he turns to inspect it, he cannot detect movement.

Lukas smiles somberly at the ridiculousness of allowing himself to indulge in such irrational fantasies. Somewhere in a level of his consciousness that's buried deeply enough to count as the truth, he realizes his death won't hold any more significance for others than his life has. It would be a lie to suggest that any part of what he's about to do is for the benefit of anyone other than himself. But it's a lie he grants himself permission to believe. He's earned it.

A faint jingling sound, almost like homemade metal chimes, distracts him. He looks closely at the old bell, but he cannot determine where the sound is coming from. He peers down into the dark abyss of the tower beneath the bell but sees nothing.

Shrugging it off, Lukas steps to the edge of the wooden railing and takes a deep breath. With his palms flat and facing down, he extends his arms until his hands hover parallel to the ground far below. He can feel the coolness of the air, and it seems to support his hands, gently lifting them in a gracious invitation. Lukas allows himself to stall, in order to savor the feeling, for it's the closest thing he's felt to contentment in a long time. It feels like unburdened lightness. Like relief.

A shuffling commotion interrupts it.

Lukas turns halfway around and spots a door, built into the frame of the tower. Its rusted knob is jostling like it's being unlocked. How could there be a door right there behind him without his having noticed it? Lukas looks more closely. He has seen this door before, this same door, but not here. Where does it lead?

Lukas stands paralyzed with confusion, when suddenly the door begins to swing open. Before he can see her, Lukas knows who's opening the door. But it doesn't make any sense. She isn't connected to this scene. What brings her here?

Lukas blinks. He shakes his head, trying to clear his thoughts. That's where he's seen the door before; it's the front door to his house. Abruptly, the cold morning air is gone. So is the sky. Lukas catches his breath, realizing that the girl is making an actual physical entrance into the house, rather than what he had at first assumed to be part of the scene being conjured in his imagination.

Katie backs in the doorway, toting an overstuffed duffel bag in one hand and an armful of vinyl records in the other, clumsily kicking the front door closed. The slamming door brings him back. He stares hazily; it takes him a minute to fully process what he's seeing. Now he remembers. He's sitting on his unimpressive sofa. There's no bell, no tower. No end in sight. His tour of duty continues. He feels a slight pang of resentment toward Katie, for interrupting what had been such a pleasant reverie, but his ill temper is fleeting. Damn her irrefutable appeal.

Katie had informed him yesterday that she was going to start moving some of her things in this morning. But she had said ten, and that had been two hours and four whiskeys ago. Perpetually late. One of those. Lukas almost makes a comment, but decides against it. Late Kate. No need to berate. Instead he offers to help. But she's okay; she's only got a few things with her today. Regardless, he shuffles over toward her anyway, light-headed, as if her youth were magnetic.

Katie smiles. She avoids looking him in the eyes, then hands him the stack of records. "You could take these if you wouldn't mind."

He stares at the records. Someone he used to know was crazy about records. "Do people still listen to records?" he asks, and his voice sounds incredibly distant.

"Not a lot of people; but I do. Some music just sounds better on vinyl." She's right. Lukas knows it, and so does she. But you're always right when you're twenty-one years old. She doesn't look a day older than twenty-one, now that she's dry. Her wiry shoulders, her posture,

29

her windblown dark brown hair—nothing's been beaten today, dragged down by serious rain or gravity. Forces like gravity are persistent; they'll get you sooner or later. Hopefully much later for Katie. So far, gravity hasn't even made a dent.

Lukas feels his face flush. He forces his attention away from the girl and examines the worn records in his arms. Flipping through the small stack, he stops, catching his breath. At once, he feels completely sober. As if he'd been smacked hard in the face. Monk. *Straight, No Chaser.* The faded cover, as familiar as the face of a dollar bill, makes Lukas remember the Hi-Fi stereo system that he treasured above all else, until the night he pushed it out a second-story window during a thunderstorm. Lukas squeezes his eyes shut, struggling to wring the memories from his mind.

It all comes rushing back anyway. Monk. The stiff fingers, searching, not deciding which note to strike until the last possible second. The wool cap. The way he'd get up and dance in the middle of a song, as if the music had taken him captive, transported him somewhere divine. The music. Lukas snaps his eyes open, flabbergasted to realize he can no longer remember the melody to a single song. It had been his most cherished album, only a mere lifetime ago.

"Do you listen to jazz," Katie asks. She is standing close to him, as if she is ready to catch him if he starts to fall over.

He's not sure he won't. "I used to," he mumbles. Lukas feels her eyes on him, asking him to elaborate. His head bobs awkwardly from side to side as he carefully chooses the right words. "I don't really listen to music anymore," he explains. "Kind of lost my taste for it."

Katie nods. "I know what you mean."

Lukas inwardly flinches at the absurdity of the statement. He knows she meant only to be polite, yet she had said it with such an odd sense of conviction. Impossible as it seems, Lukas wonders if maybe she could actually understand, were he to take the time to explain. He shrugs off the notion, dismissing it as ridiculous. He won't explain, and she won't know what he means. Lukas has settled into a routine in which he does not encounter many people during the course of an average day. The subtleties and nuances of making small talk are lost to him now. He has grown rusty with his use of the English language, and he decides not to attach too much significance to anything this young girl says. Still, there is something very unusual about her. He clears his throat and focuses on tangibles. "You're a music major, right?"

There's the lopsided smile again. "For now."

Lukas searches her face, her faraway eyes—bloodshot and warm brown. He's not sure what he's looking for, but he feels something. An image of the somber young couple from the bar last night pops into his mind, and it makes him shiver. "For now?" he repeats, slightly louder than he had intended. "Thinking of changing?"

"Not many people can make a living as a pianist." Her gaze has strayed far away from the room in which they stand.

The words don't sound like hers. "But are you one of them?" he says, immediately regretting his impulse to prolong the conversation.

Her eyes enter the present, and they seem to look through his own, to someplace deeper. Lukas is jolted by her stare, frightened to suspect that she may actually be able to see into that place that he keeps so carefully hidden.

She hesitates for a flicker of a moment, dropping her gaze. "I'm not sure I'm ready to find out," she says, in a voice that is small and brave.

Chapter Five

The coffee mug shatters against the kitchen tile. Lukas cringes. He hopes the sound didn't wake Katie up. It is a college student's inalienable right to sleep later than 8:13 a.m. on a Saturday.

Morning is always a ragged time of day for Lukas, and some are worse than others. When he is able to sleep, he sleeps severely, dreaming unsettling and shuddering images. But when he awakes, he can't remember them. He is left only with a vague sense of anxiety. An unspecific notion that something is wrong and must be put right. Unrested, he faces each new day with the daunting task of finding solutions to problems he's unable to name.

Lukas leans against the counter, trying to hold still, listening for movement in the room above him. He looks at the pieces of the mug. *Congratulations from the Palmieri Geological Survey Center. 10 years of service.* Hardly a record, but broken nonetheless. All over the kitchen floor.

Lukas decides to wait before trying to pour the coffee. He grabs the brush and copper dustpan from the closet and sweeps up the ceramic shards. He tries carrying the dustpan with both hands but still loses a piece while rattling over to the wastebasket. It's no use. The shaking in his hands has its own agenda today. He could set off a seismograph. There's no way he can hold a hammer like this. Lukas reaches for the newly replaced handle on the cabinet above the sink. The whiskey cabinet.

He unscrews a bottle of Jameson and greedily inhales its distinct aroma, at once caustic and redolently mellow. He feels his twitching nerves immediately begin to calm. It smells like reassurance.

***

Twenty minutes later, Lukas arrives with a thermos of coffee at his mother's house. He doesn't even wince at the sight of Susan's Tempo. After a while, you get used to seeing things you don't like.

And if you don't, just get rid of all the mirrors.

Susan is in the kitchen, wearing a gray wool jacket. She is drying her hands on a frayed dishtowel. "Good morning Luke," she says, unwittingly stiffening her posture.

"Hi, Susan."

"I was just about to make some coffee."

With his now-steady right hand, Lukas produces the thermos, clanging it down on the counter. "Thanks, I already have some." He heads for the living room. "Gladys awake?"

"She's not here. I just dropped her off at the hairdresser. She'll be there for about an hour."

Lukas stops, but he doesn't turn around. The walls feel much closer as the morning's light streams in through the room's squinting blinds. The hairdresser. Undoubtedly Susan's idea. "I told her I'd come by and fix those shutters today," he says quietly.

"Luke, can I ask you something?"

Should have spiked the coffee. "Sure," comes the too-quick answer.

"Nobody will tell me anything," Susan says, stepping around the counter and closer to Lukas. "How bad is it?"

Lukas rubs his eyes, immediately thinking of roughly a thousand other places he'd rather be. "It's bad."

"She's dying, isn't she?"

Focusing on tangibles, Lukas grabs his tool belt off a chair in the corner of the room. "We all are," he groans.

He heads for the front door. He knows his mother will not be alive forever, but he remains steadfast in his unwillingness to think about the subject. Nor will he ponder the mixed emotions it raises within him. He's like a child convinced that monsters lurk behind the closed doors of a closet, who refuses to fling the doors open, certain that the reality will somehow be more terrifying than his imagination.

"Lukas!"

Twenty years coagulate. No one but Susan could ever say his name and make it sound like that. It freezes him. "She's the closest thing I have to a mother," Susan blurts. "I know you can't stand to share oxygen with me, and I'm sorry about that, but this is how it has to be for now."

Lukas nods. "I gotta go fix those shutters."

"Luke, is this how it's going to stay?" The tiny muscles in Susan's cheek twitch. "Because sooner or later, neither one of us is going to have anybody left in this world. And it's going to be a pretty lonely place if we can't even talk to each other."

Lukas clenches his jaw. He turns until he almost faces her. His near-whispered words are measured, fatalistic. "It already is."

She takes another step toward him, reaches for him. He backs away. It was nonchalant, but deliberate. Susan sighs; her voice grows moist. "Luke, do you think a day goes by when I don't wish I could take it all back? I'm living with it too, you know. The fact is, you can hate me for the rest of your life if you want, but it's not going to bring Stephen back."

Lukas reaches around her and retrieves his thermos from the counter. He does not meet her pleading gaze. "It's not you I hate, Susan."

On Lukas's way out, the clanging smack of the screen door against its frame decisively signals the end of the cumbersome conversation.

Chapter Six

A renowned painting by French impressionist Georges Seurat, entitled "Sunday Afternoon on the Island of La Grande Jatte," depicts a leisurely scene of various 19th century working class people relaxing and picnicking on a sunny summer's day. At first, nothing in particular may seem to stand out. The painting's inhabitants are looking in multiple directions, seemingly at ease with, or perhaps unaware of, each other's presence. Most focus their attention to the left, toward a lake. Others gaze off to the right, but none look straight out from the canvas, which further adds to the illusion that the painting's subjects are not only unaware of each other, but also of the viewer.

Upon closer inspection, however, astute observers will notice that one of the characters in the painting is decidedly different from the rest. Seurat was known for his use of pointillism, which places tiny dots of different hues of paint close together so that when viewed from a distance the dots seem to mix and produce a richly saturated color. This enormous masterpiece—which measures over six feet by ten feet—was rendered entirely in this unique style. With the exception of one figure.

A little girl wearing a white dress and a sunbonnet appears in the exact center of the composition, and has been painted with flat brushstrokes rather than dots. She is also the only character who appears to stare directly at the viewer. The effect is unsettling, and it is what seized the attention of Katie Reiker when she first viewed the painting while on a field trip to the Art Institute during her junior year of high school.

Presently Katie is seated inconspicuously on a stool in the corner opposite the service bar at O'Malley's Pub. A half-full glass of gin, tonic, and melted ice is gathering condensation in front of her as she sits, her chin resting in her left palm as her elbow leans on the dark, sticky surface of the bar. The place is hazy with lingering cigarette smoke, overcrowded for a weeknight, but it's in a college town, so no one seems to notice. Katie's right hand idly stirs the remains of ice cubes in her drink as she mentally envisions the painting that has since become one of her favorites. She vividly recalls the moment over five years ago when she first noticed the little girl in white. It had been an odd sensation, like having been discovered while trying to hide. As she stared at the figure for what may have been hours, Katie grew more and more convinced that the artist had been trying to communicate something to the viewer through the little girl, some sense of displacement, a forlorn loneliness that seemed incongruous with her pleasant and serene environment.

Tonight once again, Katie identifies with the little girl in white, feeling alone and silent in a room that is crowded and noisy. Katie is never sure what triggers these occasional bouts of melancholy, but many times she has stood inches from her oversized Seurat poster, peering into the expression she swears can almost make out in the indistinct face of the little girl. Even holding securely to her mother's hand as they make their way through the lakeside park, the little girl seems to plead with the minions of unknown viewers to understand that she is not where she belongs.

This time her mood might have been influenced by the arrival of Eric Rollins, who entered through the front door several minutes ago and had pretended not to see her. Eric was a close friend of Kevin, who had transferred from the university this semester after he and Katie had broken up last winter. Kevin, who Katie tries valiantly never to think about. Kevin, who Katie might have loved, and may still. They weren't right for each other, and Katie is certain of this even if she can't explain it, but now, even months later, she remains plagued by a constant nagging suspicion of having somewhere gone wrong.

Despite enduring her mother's frequent impromptu sermons about the necessity for a young woman to find a suitable man, Katie has not had many boyfriends in her young life thus far. For someone with her background, she is understandably uncomfortable around most men. In the few relationships she's had, Katie has recognized early the futility of pursuing them with any real allegiance. Her mother had often warned her that authentic relationships don't just "happen," that they must be crafted through hard work and—if necessary—compromise. But Katie isn't so sure. Whatever spark existed in the romances she'd seen portrayed in movies and literature simply hadn't been there for her. Not with any of them.

Not even Kevin, she has admitted to herself, although with him she felt that she had come closest to what her friends and her mother considered to be genuine normalcy in a relationship with a man. Not that Katie truly understands what normalcy is, at least in the aspects of love. She definitely doesn't buy into her mother's theory of grit, determination, and struggle. To Katie it seems that two people should be together simply because they wish to be, because they enjoy each other's company. It doesn't seem logical that being one-half of a couple should be just another task to accomplish, like a stack of paperwork that needs to be finished.

Katie's mother had taken a keen interest in her relationship with Kevin, asking about him every time they spoke to one another, and often hinting without much subtlety at the prospects of an impending wedding, a notion that Katie would vehemently rebuke. She has never subscribed to the necessity of the institution of marriage, insisting that a legitimate relationship does not need a piece of paper to validate its veracity. Of course, this is just another of her "radical liberal viewpoints" that keep her constantly at odds with her mother, whose own beliefs have inexplicably grown more conservative and staunchly traditional with the implosions of each of the myriad ludicrous relationships she has navigated through since the failure of her marriage to Katie's father.

Katie had assumed that the feelings of loss and sense of detachment were normal after the breakup with Kevin. They would be temporary, sure to evaporate once she got involved with someone else, regardless of the level of seriousness it entailed. As it turns out, Katie has not been able to test her theory, because she has not so much as been out on a date since Kevin. And so the loneliness has stayed with her, leaving her unsure whether she misses having Kevin, or whether she just misses having someone.

Most of the time, however, Katie's "blues" — as she calls them — have nothing to do with Kevin. Nothing to do with anyone, really, other than herself and her own neuroses. Just a quirk in her genetic makeup, she supposes, the vague suspicion that once there was something that she had — she cannot remember what it was — but now it's missing. She is the little girl in white. Somehow misplaced, but uncertain where she is supposed to be.

It is a feeling as familiar as it is mysterious, something that has been with her ever since she can remember, even before the terrible events of her eighth year. It's not something she talks about with others; she had always managed to stay on top of it and keep it subdued without much strain. But always it remained. If it began to ache, it could be soothed through music. When Katie sat down at a piano, she and the instrument coaxed from one another melodies fused with delicacy and redemption. It was as if she could follow an unseen path that began at the keys of a piano and led to a place where everything made sense, and became beautiful. The piano was more potent than any drug or self-help book.

At least, it always had been.

Katie now sits, consumed by a loneliness so immense that it almost seems to be a physical presence, a shadow looming behind her. Sighing, she tips her glass and swallows the watery remains of her drink. She stands, pries some wrinkled bills from her jeans pocket, and lays them gently on a dry spot on the bar. As she makes her way toward the exit, Katie feels oddly invisible, like a shadow fading beneath the setting sun. Perhaps, she reasons, music is just a prescription in a different sort of bottle. One whose expiration date is fast approaching.

Chapter Seven

There are places you can only go alone.

In the dark place, Lukas can still hear every cricket, but what he smells is the musky interior of a brand-new 1981 Honda Civic hatchback. The radio has been turned off. The headlights make a weak attempt at stabbing a path through the rainy, foggy spring night, but Lukas can see the approaching silhouette of the bridge. He feels the car accelerate. Hears the engine race.

Keys jingle in the deadbolt lock on the front door, and Lukas is whisked back to the present. No lights are on, and he's welded to the parlor sofa, in baggy workpants and a T-shirt that's now dampened with anxious perspiration. The stealthy crickets maintain their silence until Katie is inside, closing the door behind her. Half illuminated by the invading light from the porch, she stops at the foot of the stairs. Timid, she squints into the dark parlor and says, "Mister Willow?"

"Hi ,Katie," he says, in a tone that even sounds mechanical to himself.

She steps gingerly toward the parlor, as if she were off-limits in a hospital ward. "Is everything okay?" she says. The concern in her voice induces a squirm from Lukas that even her lopsided smile has yet to do.

"I have trouble sleeping, sometimes."

Katie's shoulders drop an inch or two. "Would you mind some company," she asks, feeling her way through the dark room to the recliner.

Yes and no, he thinks. "Of course not," he says.

His eyes having long ago adjusted to the darkness, Lukas notices the graceful fashion in which Katie's delicate body settles into the oversized chair. Though it's too dark to see it, Lukas thinks of the partnerless dimple that appears on Katie's left cheek each time she smiles.

"It's not a good night for sleeping, I guess," she says. "I left the bar over an hour ago, but I knew I wouldn't be able to sleep yet."

Late-night Katie. Although he's not surprised she left the bar. You don't meet a girl like Katie in bars. "What have you been doing?"

"I went to the park," she says after a thoughtful pause. "Ever go to the park at night?"

"Not in a long time."

"It's beautiful. I like to watch the swans sleeping." Lukas can hear her smile. She draws up one slender leg and folds it under the other. "You know how people throw coins into the lake and make wishes during the day?" Lukas nods. "When I go to the park at night, I like to throw my troubling thoughts in there, instead of wishes," Katie says, cocking her head to look off to a dark corner of the room. "It seems like a good place to leave them." She snorts. "I guess that sounds kind of silly," she says, suddenly sounding self-conscious.

Lukas notices he is smiling, and it surprises him, because that's not usually what he does on this sofa. She is a very peculiar girl. "Sounds a little easier said than done is how it sounds," he says.

"Everything is."

Touché. "What was troubling you?"

Katie shrugs, looks down at her lap. She hesitates for a long moment before she answers, causing Lukas to fear that his question was too personal. "Different things, I suppose," she finally replies to Lukas's great relief. "I saw an old friend of my ex-boyfriend's at the bar tonight. Got me thinking about a lot of things."

"What happened?" Lukas says, too quickly.

"We just grew apart, I guess. We were always pretty much total opposites, but in the end, I think he just couldn't deal with the amount of time I spent alone, you know—with my music."

"Ah." Lukas nods. Common territory. "You told me the other day you were thinking of getting out of music.. Does this have anything to do with it?"

"Not directly, I don't think. But something like that definitely gets you thinking, you know? About what exactly you're willing to sacrifice for what you want. And if you really want it."

"Did you love him?" Lukas ventures. His heart momentarily stops. Had he truly said that out loud? Let alone the inappropriately personal nature of the question, the word itself had sounded awkward and foreign when it crossed his lips.

Amazingly, Katie doesn't appear bothered by the question. If she has walls, Lukas hasn't reached any of them yet. "Kevin was a great guy," she says. "I made my best mistakes with him."

She shakes her head and smiles toward the corner of the room. That lopsided smile that Lukas sees even when she's not around. She looks over at him. "What about you?"

He's startled. He has no idea what she's talking about. "Wh-what?"

His response seems to have rattled her. She stiffens her posture, and Lukas imagines he sees her blush in the darkened room.

"I mean—you know, I just meant, have you ever been married or anything?"

Lukas shakes his head. "I'd never do that to somebody," he says in the ironic tone he has perfected over the years, one which allows him to speak truthfully while passing it off as facetiousness.

"I know what you mean," Katie says.

Again, he wonders if maybe she could. Lukas feels his head grow heavy. Katie doesn't seem real. Not in this place and time, at least. She is more like a relic from a world he used to know. Since first meeting her, conversation has begun to flow from him. He does not stumble over his words, nor misconstrue hers. Well, at least not nearly as often as he does with others. It is altogether too easy to share her company, and it unnerves him. A thought flickers through his swirling consciousness. Perhaps his self-imposed isolation has finally warped his mind. Maybe she's not really here. Maybe this impossibly intuitive young woman is merely a figment of his imagination, a device conjured by his subconscious as an antidote for loneliness. Lukas grinds his jaw, swallowing away the disconcerting notion. He concentrates in order to keep his head from visibly swiveling on his neck like a bobblehead doll's, but he is now struggling to follow the course the conversation has taken. "What do your parents think about you giving up music?" he says, unsure if the question is a logical follow-up to whatever had just been said.

She takes a moment to respond. "It's just me and my mom," she says. "If I told her I was considering it, it would probably make her day. She was a singer when she was younger, but she never made anything of it, really. She sang in clubs and stuff, but not exactly what she was hoping for, you know? All those years of auditions without success sort of turned her bitter, I guess." She hesitates, as if there were more to say, but she can't find the words. Ever brave, she tries anyway. "I suppose she doesn't want me wasting years of my life the way she did. She wants me to be a nurse or something. You know, career, husband, picket fence, the whole nine yards." She crosses her arms, then crosses them the other way. Her back stiffens and her voice with it. "It's ... things with my mom are just kind of complicated."

Lukas tries to imagine what sort of person Katie's mother is, what she looks like. But all he can visualize is his own mother, wrinkled and frail. Needy, yet powerful. Lukas begins to feel the peculiar sensation again—the itch—but this time he doesn't fight it. His vision clouds. He is drifting now, somewhere between reality and the dark place. He feels as if he is seated on the other side of the room, watching himself hold this conversation with Katie the way Ebenezer Scrooge witnessed scenes from his own past. "And now," he watches himself say, "all of a sudden, you think she might be right?"

"About music for a career?" She hesitates, but doesn't wait for clarification. "I don't know," she continues, softer. "Sometimes I think if I did quit music, me and my mom could maybe start to get along." She pauses for a moment, then smiles, and continues slightly more loudly. "But I never want to be that girl, you know, the girl who makes decisions based on whether or not my mom will approve of me. That's just not me." She shoots a glance toward Lukas then returns her gaze to her lap.

"Plus, I happen to exist here in the real world, which is not something that my mom is burdened by."

Lukas nods, trying to mask his alarm at her reference to existing in the *real world*. "Hmmm," he says, feeling like a dolt. Something familiar is there, but he's not sure he recognizes it.

"So that's not the reason I've been thinking of changing majors. See, it's more than that. Sometimes it feels like ... the music is leaving me," she says, her forehead creasing. She turns away sheepishly. "I suppose that sounds a little weird."

Lukas frowns. "Not really."

His thoughts swirling, Lukas finds it difficult to draw breath. He tries to force himself to focus, to kill the sensation before it takes him over. So far, he is able to stay in the room, at least partially. *Katie is real, and so is this conversation,* he repeats to himself. Lukas is growing agitated, increasingly unsure what has been said aloud and what he has only imagined.

Katie runs her fingers through her hair, but not in the typical way. She runs them straight down, vertically from her forehead, like a comb, partially covering her face. Lukas interprets it as a nervous gesture, and he's angry with himself for making her feel uncomfortable.

She says in a soft voice, "I talk too much."

"No," Lukas fumbles. "No, not really. Not at all."

She sighs. "The thing is, it's coming down to crunch time. There's this thing at school called the Senior Showcase—"

Lukas's nodding head interrupts her.

And like a pressure valve that has just been released, Lukas's head abruptly clears. His vision is focused. He feels no itch, as if instantly awaking in full sobriety. He clears his throat weakly. "Yeah, I know about Senior Showcase," he says. "I was a music major myself when I was at the University."

"You were?" Katie pauses, as if hoping for more details. But all she gets is an expressionless stare, so she averts her eyes and says, "Then you probably know about the rigorous process of applying for a spot—all the auditions and the pressure of being evaluated by the faculty and board. And you probably also know the improbability of being one of the three students that are actually picked to perform."

Lukas nods slowly. He tries to adopt an instructive tone. "I also know how many musical careers have been jump-started by great performances at Senior Showcase." Names without faces from the past flood Lukas's mind. One young man went on to compose musical scores for motion pictures; he won an Oscar. Someone else became the first female orchestra leader for some prestigious East Coast city's symphony company. Others headed for the West Coast and became successful session players. Suddenly, as Lukas's mind clears, he now grows angry. He feels ridiculous, pretending to give advice. He hadn't planned on having to make conversation tonight, and he feels embittered toward Katie for drawing him into it.

"So you think I should apply?"

"It doesn't matter what I think," he snaps, "because I don't know anything." State a simple truth, and leave the scene. He doesn't feel like talking anymore. Keep the pressure hidden. He shivers, catching a whiff of a glass of Scotch that hasn't been poured yet. He stands, somewhat dizzy, but Katie sits, expectantly, waiting for a better answer. He can feel her expectations, and expectations usually make him hostile, but for some reason he finds his lips preparing to utter more audible words. Despite his feeling silly, this strange young woman somehow makes him want to try to find the right ones.

Indeed, more unrehearsed words spill out: "All I'm saying is, before you give up on your music, think about your old boyfriend. Think about how you might feel if you did the same thing with your music. Anything you want in life, you have to turn your back on something else."

The last two words are said while in motion. It may have made sense, and it may not have. He will have time to analyze and critique whatever it was that he's just said as soon as he's safely in his room, far away from Confusing Katie.

Chapter Eight

The sun is almost directly overhead when Lukas spots the lazy sensor. It's installed another fifty or so yards up the side of the mountain, and Lukas remembers why he doesn't monitor this one as often as he should. Of all the seismograph sensor installations under Lukas's supervision, this one is positioned at the highest elevation, a grueling fifteen-minute hike nearly straight up from the spot where the mountain road ends. The spot where Lukas's Volvo now sits, no doubt amused at its owner's pitiful cardiovascular condition. Letting his pack drop to his side, he stops and props one foot up on a monument-sized rock while he surveys the valley to his left. A steady wind sways the treetops, making the forest below him resemble the undulating waves of the ocean. No matter which direction he turns, the wind seems to try to repel him, making his climb more arduous, as if the depleted air at this altitude weren't bad enough. His nose is running, whether from the elevation or the falling temperature he's not sure. Lukas stands beneath a cloudless sky, and he can see all the way across the next county. The oil derricks look no bigger than Tinker Toys. They don't seem so impressive from up here. Or from down there, depending on who you talk to.

Lukas sucks in a lungful of air and continues his climb. He's been putting this trip off ever since the sensor stopped registering readings in his office four days ago. He looks up the hill at it, and shakes his head. Each one of the twelve remote sensor installations that Lukas is responsible for—he calls them the "dirty dozen"—look exactly like this one, except the other eleven actually work. The part that protrudes above ground resembles a shiny, overturned half-sphere fastened to a tripod, like some shabby prop spaceship from an old science fiction film. They function like remote seismographs; each is equipped with tiny hanging weights enclosed inside the shiny, solid frames that connect to a shaft buried deep into the ground. The weights stay stationary, and they record any movement within the earth's crust by the motion of the glossy frame that surrounds them. Then they send their data via telephone wires back to the antique seismograph in Lukas's office, which prints out the results as endless sets of zig-zagging blue lines across miles and miles of reams of paper. Technically the printouts are called seismograms, but to Lukas they look more like an EKG chart for the planet, and they use up a forest's worth of paper every week. The cramped office and the piles of paper do not bother Lukas, but the physical exertion required for the maintenance of these remote sensors is another matter entirely. *Some people do this sort of hiking for recreation,* Lukas reminds himself. Then again, some people like to cut themselves. Crazy is as crazy does.

Lukas hopes it's just a faulty beacon gauge, or something wrong with the radio transmitter. That's all the more serious a malfunction he's equipped to fix today, and he'll be damned if he's making this hike for nothing. More than likely the sensor just got bored, somehow realizing the insignificance of its duty at this altitude. It's jammed into a slab of continental crust that's probably fifty miles thick under this mountain. If anything deep down started to dance, this little guy would be the last one to know about it. But that's no excuse. It was installed to perform a task. No matter how completely one loses interest, there are still obligations that need to be met.

Lukas stops. He turns and looks down at the world beneath him, sensing something's not right. He starts to feel the *itch*. He shudders, recalling his ungraceful conversation with Katie last night. But today the itch feels different. He calls it an "itch" because the word "clairvoyance" would get strange looks from people. Not that he's ever spoken to anyone about it, nor does he plan to. It frightens him to think about, and exasperates him to try to understand, so he does his best to keep it at bay. But it's there. It's been lurking inside of him for over twenty years now, appearing without beckoning and with no forewarning. And it's never wrong.

He unclips the pager from his belt and looks it over. Sure enough, in less than ten seconds it starts to beep.

***

Supporting the weight of his head in his hands, Lukas notices for the first time how far back on his scalp his hairline begins. It's hard not to think about the effects of age while sitting in a hospital room. His forehead feels warm, his skin stretched too tightly. He must have gotten more sun than he'd planned on during his hike this morning.

"False alarm, kiddo."

His mother's weak voice surprises him. Lost alone in his dark places, he'd assumed she was sleeping. He gingerly slides his chair closer to her bedside. "How you feeling, Gladys," he asks.

She shrugs, in slow motion. "Ready to go, I suppose. Just not today." She leans her head forward and looks at him sideways. "How 'bout you?"

Lukas stands. "Today's as good a day as any, I guess," he says, slipping into his trademark ironical tone. He walks to the window, opens the blinds, and looks up at the mountain, grand in the afternoon sun. At that lazy sensor he never quite reached. He feels a flare of indignation blaze through him. You can't just quit because you get bored! The worst part is, he'll have to repeat that vexing hike tomorrow, against the relentless wind. Lukas cringes at the thought. Better take along a thermos.

"It never turns out the way you think it might," the old woman says. His back to her, Lukas braces himself. He hates it when she starts to reminisce. "I'll tell you, Luke, your daddy and me, we were gonna see the world." She emits a fluttering sound that might be a chuckle. "You'd have liked him. He was like you when you were younger, always thinking big. Always a step or two away from greatness." Lukas doesn't have to turn around to see her smile, the same one that always shows up on her face when she recalls the fictional character known as his father. "What he lacked in common sense, boy, he made up for with dreams. Just talking, he could get you so excited, so inspired. And that's a rare trait in a man. That's what I loved about him, I guess." She pauses among her memories, still smiling. "I suppose that's also why I was always such a sucker for you, kiddo."

Turning from the window but still not looking directly at her, Lukas says, "Did you really believe I could have been great?"

The old woman's mouth drops open. She stares with an expression of disbelief. "You still can, Luke!" Her withered mouth forms a jumble of silent syllables until the next audible ones come out: "It wasn't the music that mattered. I never cared about that. I'd love you no matter how you decide to live."

Lukas faces her. His expression is blank, but inwardly he seethes, resenting all the unfair circumstances that allow such a fragile human being to wield such power. And immediately he curses himself for having such feelings about the woman that gave him the gift of life. The gift that he is stuck with, one that he cannot possibly return. Well, at least not for as long as her reign endures.

"But the catch is, you have to decide to live," she adds, smiling a wrinkled, knowing smile. "Just being alive isn't enough, kiddo."

And she may be right. But it's more than Stephen got to do.

Chapter Nine

Five more minutes, Katie decides. *Then I'm outta here.*

It's early September, and the weather is extremely hot for this time of year. The temperature in the alcove where Katie waits fluctuates greatly, depending on which door swings open. She is crammed as far as she can fit into the corner, on a vinyl padded sofa-bench in the anteroom of Alberto's, her favorite local Italian restaurant. When people enter or exit through the door leading outside, the day's muggy air puffs in, unpleasantly filling the tiny area like the breathy exhalation of someone standing too close to your face. Relief comes almost instantly, as the door to the restaurant's interior opens, allowing cool, air-conditioned air to spill out into the waiting area, along with the distant sounds of Dean Martin. Or possibly Tony Bennett; Katie has always had trouble telling the two apart. The backs of her thighs stick to the vinyl seat, and she lifts one leg at a time, slowly peeling them free for a moment, then decides to cross her legs.

Another waiting area is situated just inside the door, beside the hostess station, in the part that's air-conditioned. Katie chooses to stay put, away from the view of the hostesses and servers that linger idly, waiting for the lunch rush to begin. She does not want an audience to witness her growing agitation and mounting embarrassment as each minute ticks away and leaves the appointed meeting time for lunch further and further in the past. Five more minutes until it's officially declared a no-show, Katie thinks, chewing on her lip in irritation, and then it's Wendy's drive-through for lunch. And another patch woven neatly into what is becoming the defining pattern of her life.

It's more annoyance than disappointment. At least that's what she tries to convince herself of as she runs her fingers through her newly-cut hair for the millionth time today. Maybe she shouldn't have gotten quite so much taken off. Maybe then she wouldn't be so self-conscious. Maybe then she could be waiting inside the comfortable restaurant, unconcerned whether or not the staff is taking silent bets on how long it takes until she acknowledges that she's been stood up and leaves. The haircut was supposed to make her feel more confident, not less. It was supposed to help her project how self-reliant she is, how she's not just getting by on her own, but thriving, and that she'd be damned if she needs to impress anyone to feel good about herself. Katie is always disgusted by her insecurities. Only the weak make crutches out of their pasts and limp through the present. And Katie is not weak; she is resilient, and she does not look back. But if she had just left the hair a little bit longer. Just a couple of lousy inches.

She checks her watch again and snorts, shaking her head. Deciding it's been long enough and that she doesn't need the aggravation, she uncrosses her legs, snatches up her pocketbook, and stands. Just then the door to the outside swings open. Sunlight and balmy air barge into the alcove. Katie stops, letting out a breath and allowing her shoulders to sag.

There, in the doorway, huffing as if she's just expended slightly more energy than a human being could be expected to part with, stands Katie's mother. Twenty-seven minutes late.

Once seated, Katie and Nora are handed menus by a perky, redheaded waitress named Tiffany, who looks to be a couple of years younger than Katie. She chirps that she'll be right back with some ice water for them, and when she walks away, Nora leans in conspiratorially.

"The traffic around here has become simply treacherous," she says in a harsh whisper. "Some of these people have *no business* being behind the wheel of an *automobile*. I remember when this used to be such a lovely little town."

Katie purses her lips and nods. "Ah. You mean the last time you came to visit. Well, a lot can change in three years."

"Really, Katherine, don't be so dramatic. It hasn't been that long at all." As she speaks, Nora's eyes scan across the room, pausing briefly on each of the few table areas where other patrons are seated.

Katie shakes her head as an implacable smirk flashes across her face. "Yes, Mother, actually it has," she says, allowing her voice to trail off as she flips her menu open. "But then, why would you ever take my word for anything?"

Nora glares at her. "I'll not have that conversation again." Her words are icy. Katie looks up briefly, opens her mouth as if to reply, but wilts beneath her mother's hard stare. She sighs and goes back to scanning the menu, inwardly seething at her mother's use of the word *again* when she had never even deigned to allow the conversation to take place a first time.

"At any rate, if it weren't for the traffic I'd have been here earlier."

Nora's face is flushed, and she fans herself with one hand. She seems to be uncomfortably warm, but Katie silently predicts that she will not take off the inexpensive-looking white blazer, or the scarf she has tied fashionably around her collar. Nora has always been fond of scarves; she says wearing them makes her feel debonair, which is not the first word Katie would choose to describe them.

Without taking her eyes off the menu, Katie says, "So what inspired you to make such a long drive today?" Her affronted tone makes her frame of mind obvious.

Nora pretends not to notice. She picks up her own menu and flips immediately to the back page. She squints at the small print. Katie knows her mother can't read what's printed on the menu. She thinks her reading glasses make her look old, so she hasn't worn them since the day she got them. "Well, you said you had something you wanted to talk to me about, didn't you?" she says, acting as if she's reading the menu.

"Yes, but ordinarily we talk over the phone. What makes today so special?"

Nora looks up at her daughter with wide, uncomprehending eyes. "Well, it sounded like it must have been something important."

Katie's inability to respond goes unnoticed as the smiling, bubbly waitress arrives at the table and places a tall glass of ice water in front of each of them. "There you go," she says. "Something to cool you off on such a muggy day. Could I start you--?"

"Thank you dear," Nora says, a hand flipped in the air. "And could you also bring me a vodka martini, extra dry with a twist, as soon as you can possibly get a chance?"

Tiffany smiles, turning to Katie. "And for you?"

Katie does not take her eyes off her mother. "I'm fine with water. Thank you." Once the waitress has receded out of earshot, Katie says, "Mother …"

"Katherine," Nora says, mocking her tone playfully. She leans forward and clasps her hands. "So, tell me what's new. You said you found a place to live, right? Tell me all about it. Any new men in your life?" She smiles a mischievous grin.

Katie feels her jaw muscles clench. She knows precisely where this conversation is headed, and she's having none of it. She tucks her too-short hair behind her ear and turns her attention back to the menu. "Men are the least of my worries right now, Mother."

Nora's smile hardens, and she looks down at her menu. "Well, you just haven't found the right one yet."

Katie rolls her eyes. "Now this is the argument I don't want to have today—"

"Who's arguing?" Nora says, an expression of astonishment on her face. Katie doesn't respond. "We'll talk about something else then," she says, turning back to the front of her menu, and squinting at it. "What else is happening? Any exams yet … or whatever it is music majors call them?"

Katie glowers daggers at her mother, who doesn't look her in the eyes.

Tiffany returns, both hands tightly grasping a tray that bears a single, clear martini. She places it gently in front of Nora and asks if they are ready to order lunch. Nora is still concentrating on the menu, eyes squinched. "Oh my heavens," she says, looking up at the girl and ignoring the martini. "We haven't even had a moment to decide yet. Is there any way you could give us just a few more minutes?"

"Of course. Not a problem; take as long as you need." She spins and retreats toward the kitchen. The rest of her section of the restaurant is empty.

Nora watches the young waitress closely until she is all the way in the kitchen, and the wide door swings shut behind her. "Mercy," she mutters, "I am simply *dying* of thirst." Grabbing the martini, she casts a quick glance around the room and brings the drink to her lips. Instead of sipping, Nora tilts the glass toward her and in four quick swallows, the cocktail is gone.

Katie's stare is a mixture of disbelief and horror. "*Jesus*," she hisses.

"That's the way to hit the spot," Nora says, and she gives Katie a wink. "Hasn't anyone ever taught you how to drink a martini?"

"It's a little early for me," Katie mutters, slouching down slightly in her chair. She can feel her cheeks redden. Then, to her dismay, Katie watches her mother take her glass of water and carefully begin to refill the martini glass, all the while scoping the rest of the restaurant for any onlookers. Nora wipes the lip of the glass dry, replaces it in the spot where the waitress had set it down, and shoves her water glass further toward the opposite end of the table.

Katie is stupefied. "You have got to be kidding me …"

Nora ignores her, directing her full attention back to trying to read the menu as the waitress once again approaches the table.

"Have you two decided?"

Katie is seized with dread, hoping she's wrong about what she thinks will soon take place.

Nora places the menu on the table and turns to the waitress. "I believe I'll have the veal cutlet, dear." Quickly she adds, "You look about college-aged. Do you by any chance attend the university?"

Jotting the order on her pad, Tiffany smiles. "Yeah, I'm a freshman."

"Oh how wonderful," Nora says, starting to gesture with her hands as she speaks. "My daughter Katherine is just beginning her fourth year. Do you two know each other?" She motions toward Katie, who looks up meekly toward the girl.

Tiffany studies Katie's face for a prolonged moment, a polite half-smile suspended on her lips. "No," she says, still smiling.

Katie makes no response.

"Oh, she just adores it," Nora jumps in. "Don't you, dear?" With that question she reaches for Katie's hand, knocking her martini glass on its side and sending Tiffany jumping back to dodge the splash.

"Oh, good heavens!" Nora shrieks. "Oh, how embarrassing! Did I get you, did I get either of you?" She shakes the silverware out of the nearest napkin and begins to dab at the spill. "Oh what a buffoon I am!"

"Don't worry about it," Tiffany reassures her, moving the table's centerpiece away from the wet spot. "These things happen all the time, no problem." She grabs a towel from her apron and soaks up most of the mess. She takes the empty martini glass and picks up the lemon rind.

Katie shakes her head, dumfounded. She feels as if she's watching a movie, and she's embarrassed for the director.

"I am so, so sorry," Nora says with convincing sincerity.

"Not a problem at all," Tiffany says. "I'll go and grab you some more napkins, and I'll bring you a fresh drink. Just give me a second."

"Thank you, sweetheart, I'm such a dreadful klutz." Nora calls after her as she scampers toward the bar.

Katie leans in toward her mother, red-faced and seething. "I can't *believe* you did that."

"What?" comes the benign response.

"That was absolutely pathetic, Mother. I can't believe you."

"Katherine, you know they overcharge for those things," Nora whispers. "They're probably six or seven dollars apiece. I'm unemployed; I have to be careful how much I spend nowadays."

"I don't see how you possibly could —" Katie stops. She watches her mother rearrange her silverware for a moment. She arches one of her eyebrows. "Unemployed?"

Nora looks sheepish. She places her hands on her lap. "Yes. I lost my job, I'm afraid. A victim of downsizing."

"What?"

Nora's voice and demeanor soften. "I wasn't going to tell you. Not until I found something else." She looks up at Katie. "It's no big deal. I'm going to find a smaller place, something with less extravagant rent."

Katie places both elbows on the table and drops her head into her hands. "Mother, you can't make rent?"

"Now, Katherine, don't start," Nora says, her voice a whisper of admonishment, "I didn't come down here today to ask you for another loan. I came because I wanted to see you."

Katie looks up at her mother, her lips pressed firmly together. She sighs. Folds her arms one over the other. Somewhere deep inside her skull a headache is forming, like gathering storm clouds. Now she's a part of this ridiculous movie, an unwitting supporting actress.

"Don't give it another thought," Nora says. "I'll figure something out."

The young waitress comes back to the table and places a fresh martini in front of Nora, telling her in jest to be careful with this one. She turns toward Katie. "I'm sorry," she says, pulling her pad out of her apron. "I never got your lunch order. What would you like?"

Katie stares at her mother until the woman can no longer hold her gaze. Without looking up at the waitress, Katie says, "Just the water."

Chapter Ten

Lukas drops the outdated magazine onto the pile and sighs. He has just read a four-page article about an actor. Someone who played Johnny Cash in a movie. Lukas can't even recall the man's name. He had read every word of the article, even the captions, yet he cannot recollect even one detail from it. Lukas draws a deep breath and arches his back, trying to dislodge the clenched sensation he feels at the base of his rib cage. He pivots in the chair, stretching and straining to no avail. There it sits, like a smoldering wedge in his abdomen. Although more than likely it is merely his body's unwillingness to digest the second microwave cheeseburger he'd bought from the hospital vending machine, for a moment Lukas imagines himself having a heart attack, flopping over right here in the waiting room, besting his elderly mother in a race towards death.

He smiles briefly at the irony, but dismisses the notion equally as fast. Lukas tries not to think about his own motivations and desires, because invariably he seems to dislike whatever he finds out about himself. Avoiding introspection is a tough trick to pull off for a modern day hermit, but he tries valiantly. He shakes his head, recalling the conflicting emotions he'd experienced on the mountain when he'd gotten the page about his mother. There was the usual trepidation to be sure, but there was also a twinge of—what was that—hope? Lukas is disgusted by the possibility. Is that, in fact, why he still sits here waiting, despite having been encouraged several times by his mother to go home—because he is actually hoping for bad news?

Lukas is conscious of his resentment at having had to transition over the past several years into what amounted to a parental role for his own parent. No one enjoys that kind of morbid responsibility. But what kind of a person could be so morally decayed as to be capable of formulating feelings of relief at the prospect of a parent's death?

Certainly no one that he wants to hang around with, Lukas decides.

He rises from the chair and storms out of the waiting room through the sliding glass doors, and into the afternoon's fading sunlight.

***

Two hours later the sun makes its final descent below the horizon, leaving a wash of tangerine light peering out from behind a smattering of small, wispy cloud remnants. Lukas sits alone on a shabby park bench, watching the sky's trembling twin fade across the surface of the pond. Nearby, a foursome of swans keeps a watchful eye on his quivering hands as he clumsily peels open a new roll of antacid tablets. When one's diet consists of as great a portion of distilled liquids as Lukas's does, antacids are as commonplace in clothing pockets as loose change or car keys. A few scattered lightning bugs signal the coming evening, as they admire the reflections of their flashes in the pond. Lukas pops two tablets into his mouth and frowns. After he left the hospital, he had driven around numbly and ended up here at the park. Probably due to his conversation with Katie the previous night, he had sat in this spot for so long because of a subconscious desire to rid himself of his troubling thoughts. To cast them into the pond, like spare coins, and forget them.

But suddenly it occurs to him that Katie herself may show up at any minute, and how would he explain his presence to her? He would feel altogether foolish. He stuffs the antacids back into his pocket and rises stiffly to his feet. Besides, he reasons, it's not working. His troubling thoughts haven't budged an inch. Maybe the park works for Katie, but Lukas knows exactly where he needs to go.

***

The parking lot of Chadwick's Liquor Store is deserted except for two college-age boys, clearly inebriated, loudly arguing on the sidewalk about the merits of a playoff system for NCAA football. Lukas emerges from his car and shuffles past them without making eye contact.

The tinny jingle of a small brass bell announces his entrance into the otherwise silent store. The man leaning behind the counter looks up from his newspaper and flashes Lukas a friendly smile. Without counting his paces or looking around, Lukas arrives at a spot he knows well and snatches a bottle of single malt Scotch whiskey from the top shelf. If he ever has a son, Lukas decides—okay, a dog—he'll name him Glen.

Making his way to the register, Lukas fishes his wallet out of his back pocket. The cashier folds his newspaper in half, drops it on the counter, and approaches the register. He appears to be about Lukas's age, short and paunchy stout. His face is ruddy, but his eyes twinkle from behind wire-rimmed glasses as he smiles at Lukas. "Good afternoon, Mister Willow," he offers in a friendly way. "How we doin' this evening?"

Lukas slides the bottle across the counter. It can't simultaneously be afternoon and evening. He doesn't look up. "I'm okay," he mutters softly. "How are you, sir?"

The man smiles in a restrained, almost-frowning way, as if trying not to smile at a private joke, as he slides the bottle across the scanner. While stooping to grab a paper bag from beneath the counter, he looks up over the rims of his glasses at Lukas. "Sir?" he repeats, clearly amused. "You know, pretty much everybody that comes in here more than once calls me Jake," he says, indicating the spot where his name is embroidered on his Chadwick's shirt.

Weary of holding the pair of limp twenty-dollar bills between his unsteady fingers, Lukas lays them on the counter and pushes them toward the man.

"I been working here for the better part of four years," the man continues, "and I see you at least two, sometimes three times a week, Mister Willow." He smiles as he unfolds the paper bag and slips the Scotch inside. "I always wondered why you never call me by my name. 'Sir' is a little formal, don't you think?"

Lukas wishes the man would just take his cash and render him his change. He briefly considers telling him to keep the change. Instead he shrugs, and shoots a sheepish glance at the man's amused eyes. "It's just a habit, I s'pose. I guess I don't know why I do it."

Jake just grins. Lukas feels his face getting warmer. He grabs hold of the bottle, ready to make what will undoubtedly turn out to be an incredibly awkward exit.

"Well," Jake says, finally taking Lukas's money and ringing it up. "Whatever floats your boat, I guess, as the saying goes." He grabs two singles and a pile of coins from the register and drops them into Lukas's outstretched hand. "You take 'er easy, now, Mister Willow."

Lukas forces a barely serviceable attempt at a smile and hastily makes his way under the jingling bell back out into the parking lot.

It's not entirely true. Lukas knows exactly why he does it. But the reasons are myriad, and they're not uplifting. People don't want to hear the answers to the questions they ask you, not really. Not unless the answers are more of the same trivial slew of pleasantries that aimlessly float between people and pass for conversations on a daily basis. Real, genuine conversation requires sincere thought. It is taxing. It is hard work. Which is why so few people practice it.

The truth is, Lukas has no desire to get to know any more people than he already knows. Less, if he had his choice. Fewer people to have to make conversation with, to try and explain things that are not explainable. Fewer people to miss him when he's gone. Just as soon as all obligations are taken care of. Then he can exit freely and subtly, like emerging from a pool without rippling the surface. Like an extra leaving from the background of a movie scene in a crowded restaurant. Check, please.

But it's not just gaining new friends that Lukas tries to avoid.

Small talk with strangers, banter with a cab driver, sitting too close to someone at a bar—any of it can unwittingly access his special gift and lead to dire results. Acquaintances, passersby, anyone that engages him in a conversation can inadvertently burden him with their own sorrows.

Not on purpose. It just happens. He is like a sponge, soaking up the pain of those he encounters. It is something he can't explain, and something over which he has no control. He's at its mercy.

So the best he can do is to try to identify situations where it might occur and avoid them altogether. Preventative maintenance. He keeps himself distant, before he ends up knowing enough about a person to feel more than he wants to.

He's got enough of his own pain to reconcile, so he tries to dodge any circumstances that might trigger it.

Whatever it is.

The "itch" he calls it, for lack of a better term. His unique, unaccountable ability. His gift. His punishment.

Chapter Eleven

Lukas spots Katie's green Volkswagen Beetle parked along the curb as he slows down to pull into the driveway. He envies her. For her youth, her looks, her vitality. But also if she is able to pull off the trick she claims. Lukas had tried to cast his troubling thoughts in the park pond, as she'd described, but it hadn't worked. Now it appears that they've followed him home. Lukas snorts. The bastards know where he lives. With shaking hands, he shifts into park. It is high time for a drink.

Turning off the ignition, Lukas reaches over to grab the brown bag he'd brought home from the liquor store and notices his repair kit on the passenger seat. He never did get to that lazy sensor. He covers the repair kit with a newspaper, hoping he'll forget about it in the morning. Not likely, though. Lukas is cursed with a good memory, and some days are worse than others.

He trudges up the walkway to the front porch. The house is dark. Katie's keys still hang in the lock on the front door. Lukas smiles. Just like Forgetful Katie. Free-spirited, maybe. He wants to go up and scold her for leaving her keys in the door, like any good landlord would. Mostly he just wants to see her lonesome dimple. The thought makes him feel foolish, and dangerously sober, so he dismisses the notion and opens the heavy door, snatching her keys from the lock.

Katie's backpack is dumped right inside the door; library books and CDs are scattered haphazardly around the alcove's floor. This is not like Katie.

He closes the door behind him and looks up the stairs toward Katie's bedroom. Lights are off, but the door appears to be open. Lukas feels a clenching sensation take hold of his throat. Something's not right. In his peripheral vision, he spots movement in the darkened parlor to his right.

He steps over the scattered books, hears a muffled sound and then Katie's panic-streaked voice: "Help!"

Lukas reaches for the light switch, but his adrenalized mind immediately remembers the bulbs are burned out.

"Not another move!" comes an unfamiliar voice.

Lukas freezes. His eyes narrow and rapidly grow accustomed to the darkness. On the far side of the parlor, a man, not much larger than Katie, and much smaller than Lukas, has his right arm clasped tightly around the girl's neck, and he holds what is probably a gun toward her head. Lukas can hear the blood pumping through the veins in his own temples.

"He's gonna kill me!" Katie yelps.

"Shut up!" warns the man. He shifts his weight from one leg to the other, jerking Katie around like a drugged dance partner. The scene makes Lukas dizzy. He does nothing for a moment, waiting for confirmation that what he's seeing is truly taking place.

Katie is crying in the darkness. A stabbing pain flares through Lukas's forehead. It's real. The bottle of Scotch he cradles in his left arm suddenly grows impossibly heavy; his shaking becomes more exaggerated. All the moisture in his mouth immediately evaporates. He can barely say, "Who are you?"

"I'm the guy who's gonna shoot her in the face if you try anything stupid."

Lukas blinks, trying not to see double. "Why?"

The dancing stops. Apparently the question was just as unexpected to the man holding the gun as it was to the man who asked it. "What?" he says, not sounding sure whether it's okay to be confused.

Lukas's mouth starts to form the beginning of a response, then a different one, then a third, before finally some perceptible words come out. "What I mean is, why would you shoot her? You seem to have her under control already. I'm the one you're not sure about." He's not sure that made sense. Words are forming and then propelling themselves from Lukas's mouth independently while his brain scrambles for something—anything—that he should do next.

The young man points the gun at Lukas; he tightens his grip around Katie's neck, eliciting a choked squeak from her. Apparently, that was the wrong thing to say.

The stranger hisses, "You trying to hint at something, big man?"

Lukas twists his torso and flips a switch. Outside, the porch is bathed in light. Some light seeps into the house through the windows. Lukas can see his face now.

"Turn it off!" the man shouts.

Lukas doesn't move. He studies the intruder. Younger guy, maybe Katie's age, more scared than he wants to let on. And there's something else, too. Lukas can already feel that familiar itch, stronger with this one than usual. The quivering muscles in his arms and legs begin to grow numb.

"You know this guy, Katie?" Lukas says.

"He was in the house when I—" she starts, but is cut off by the python grip. The dancing starts again. Lukas feels ill, weak in the joints. His concentration is waning, but he notices the young man's wide eyes are locked in on his. Lukas is not equipped with the right qualities to be thrust into such a grave situation. Somehow this is going to end tragically, and it will undoubtedly be his fault. He is ready to concede failure. He hates himself for letting Katie down. He feels like collapsing. Preferably into a bathtub of Scotch.

"What we gonna do here, big man?" the young man says, cocking the gun like gangsters do in the movies.

The answer is obvious.

"I'm going to have a drink," Lukas says. With his right hand he reaches into the paper bag, grasps the neck of the bottle of Scotch, and lets the empty paper bag fall to the floor. "Want one?"

The arm dips, the dance stops. The gun and the stranger are dumfounded. Lukas can almost make out the expression of disbelief on Katie's face, and he's sorry. But he doesn't know what else to do.

Lukas turns toward the liquor cabinet.

"Watch it!" the young man cries. The gun arm has regained its poise, even if the man's voice hasn't. "You move one more inch and I'll shoot you. It's that simple."

Lukas nods. This is not how he had envisioned his death, but he decides that it will suffice. When he speaks, his voice is calm, almost relieved. "I'm going to open that cabinet right there and make two drinks," he says, indicating the mini-freezer. "Two Scotches, with ice. You do what you have to do, but let me just tell you this: in my experience, killing someone is not as easy a thing to forget as you might think."

He takes two steps and stands at the liquor cabinet.

"You think I'm fucking around?" the intruder blurts, clearly with more desperation than he'd have liked to let on. The gun follows Lukas, bobbing and swaying, but it holds its peace.

The overwhelming silence crowds in on Lukas's eardrums like an inflating balloon. When he sets two cocktail glasses on the marble top of the cabinet, the resulting clink is deafening. He doesn't even look over at the young man as he clumsily scoops ice into each glass. The pouring is wobbly; the full bottle feels cumbersome in Lukas's right hand. For a moment he wants to smash the bottle on the young man's forehead for making Katie cry. Maybe after this drink he'll be able to do just that. But no, something is on the way. He's not sure what; he's never sure until it gets there. But he definitely feels the itch; it feels like an itch on the inside of his skin.

Lukas turns and carries the two drinks to the coffee table and sits down on his sofa spot. He can hear Katie and the strange stranger, in a contest to see who can breathe the loudest. Lukas brings the unsteady glass to his nose and inhales the smoky scent; the skin on his forearm tingles, as if tickled by a fairy lover. The first sip is accompanied by the usual gratitude; the second calms him immensely. It helps to bring him partial understanding.

"I'm sorry I couldn't oblige you," he says humbly, finally looking back up at the young man. The gun has lost interest; it points at the floor.

The young man shakes his head brusquely, as if Lukas's liquor ritual had lulled him into some kind of trance. "Are you talking to me?" he says, irritated. His bewilderment is as evident as the features on his face.

"I'm assuming you intended to rob me," Lukas says, pausing to carefully analyze each word he speaks. He probably shouldn't be assuming anything about someone who's crazy or desperate enough to commit armed robbery. Assumption takes gumption. The crickets are silent. Katie's no longer crying. She's probably as befuddled by what's going on as the young thief. Well, that makes three of them. "I guess you've gathered by now that there's not much to steal. No TV, no stereo." He motions toward the loveseat, then toward the glass. "All I can offer you is a drink."

The young man remains planted, his arm wrapped like a vine around Katie. Lukas tries to avoid looking at her, but he can't help it. When the gunshot eventually sounds, the only thing Lukas will regret is not knowing what will happen to Katie. Even misplaced by her fear and uncertainty, she's beautiful. Skin smooth like twice-melted wax, from her face down to where it's stretched over a firm belly that barely peeks out from beneath a rumpled blue blouse. It fills Lukas with misery. An unsoiled vessel that doesn't belong in this filthy scene. The expression of terror she wears on her face feels like a knife in his chest; he finds himself wishing desperately that the young man would hurry up and shoot him. Closing his eyes, Lukas takes a long swallow, silently pleading for a gunshot. When one doesn't come, he looks wearily back at the stranger, feeling an odd serenity begin to envelop him.

Hypnotized maybe, the young man drags Katie to the loveseat and pushes her down. Then he sits beside her, looking past the drink, perhaps trying to read in Lukas's eyes an explanation for his bizarre actions.

Happy hunting, kid, but don't hold your breath.

Lukas can't stand to be stared at. He closes his eyes, so he can drink alone. He concentrates upon the itch that continues to swell within him.

When he opens his eyes, the gun has switched hands, and the boy is lifting the drink to his lips. A swallow, followed by a sharp, appalled exhale.

"Uh!" He slams the glass back down on the table. It pains Lukas to see some of it spill. "How can you drink that stuff?"

There are no such things as rhetorical questions. Plus, he already knows this one. "I guess because it's the answer," he responds without hesitation.

Ready to curse or to threaten, the young man seems to lose the words on their way out. Instead he mumbles, "It's what?"

"The answer," Lukas explains. "The answer you have to turn to because all the other answers turn out to be wrong." He leans closer to the boy. This is part of it, at least. Lukas can now see a faint vision of a house that was never a home, never big enough maybe. A girl, a maiden in distress. It's up to the knight to turn things around. "It's not fair, really," he continues, feeling slightly emboldened. "Nature should have to follow its own rules. But sometimes it doesn't."

"What the hell is wrong with you?" He looks at Katie. "What's wrong with him?"

Lukas stares straight at the boy, allowing the mist in his mind to clear. "I mean the theory of opposites. The yin and the yang, as some people call it."

Lukas draws another sip of Scotch, his eyes never wandering from the hopelessly perplexed eyes of the young man.

"Every day has its night. Every yes has its no." Lukas shrugs sadly. "So it's just not fair when you come upon a question, but there's no right answer to it. How can there not be a right answer, when there are about a million wrong answers?" He smiles humorlessly. Clear images are starting to materialize in his head now. He leans closer. "You do know what I mean. Don't you?"

"Fuck you. You don't know me."

His arm still drapes around Katie, looking almost comfortable. Almost perversely natural. Lukas feels his face flush. He can sense the boy's escalating fear. He decides to go on the offensive.

He leans forward. Pauses for a moment, as if waiting for something to happen. He whispers, "Why don't you let her go, kid? Can't you see she's better than both of us?"

The gun arm flies out from around Katie and zooms in on imaginary crosshairs on Lukas's forehead. The boy's body quivers; perhaps he is unsettled by the fact that the sudden pressure of the cold steel barrel against Lukas's head didn't evoke so much as a flinch from him.

The strange eyes narrow. Terror is quickly morphing into aggression. "Give me one reason I shouldn't kill you right now, you twisted son of a bitch."

The eyes. The itch reaches the surface. Lukas can now clearly see the pain. He can see it all, as if he'd lived it himself. He returns the young man's gaze, but his own softens.

"Because how would you explain it to your baby?" Lukas whispers.

The eyes grow wide as the color vanishes from the young man's face. As if pushed by an invisible force, he stumbles backwards against the loveseat. His momentum sends him careening to the floor. A look of sheer horror mars the young man's face as he scrambles to his feet, his eyes never straying from Lukas. Unable to breathe, the boy doesn't speak. He backs toward the front door, trips on library books. Panic gives him wings. One footstep against the porch is heard, and he's gone.

Lukas's eyes drift back to Katie. She has curled herself into a ball on the loveseat. Her body quivers as she sobs silently, her eyes squeezed shut so tightly that her face is contorted, unrecognizable. The sight is too much for Lukas to take. A dull pain, unique and terrifying, caves in his chest, and his vision blurs. He struggles to get up off the couch and move toward her. Stepping around the coffee table, he arranges himself unsteadily on top of it, facing her but unable to look directly at her. He sits completely still, having no idea what to do.

Katie's eyes open and she jerks, startled to see him sitting a few inches from her. Lukas remains welded to the coffee table, his twitching hands lying dumbly in his lap. Suddenly Katie springs up from the loveseat and starts to throw her arms around his neck.

Even in his stupor, Lukas's reflexes are stiff, refined. His arms instinctively pop up from his sides and he holds her back by the shoulders. "It—it's okay," he says, guiding her into a sitting position facing him. "Did he hurt you?"

Katie settles back onto the loveseat, hugging herself with shivering arms. She drops her gaze. "I was just going to hug you," she says, embarrassed. She sniffles softly. When she looks back at him, her expression is pleading for something, but he's not sure what.

He looks away from her troubling eyes. He can smell her sweat. Better than Scotch. He hadn't done it on purpose. He stammers, "I'm just … I'm not much of a hugger." He shudders, feeling as if his own skin were the wrong size. It was the closest he'd come to a hug in twenty years.

Katie's lips twitch. She forces a gaze back toward the door. "Should we call the police?" she says, standing uneasily.

"No. Let him go."

She studies him, but does not protest. "Why?" Her tone sounds puzzled, like a chill he wishes he could cover with a warm blanket.

Lukas stands and looks down at the inquisitive creases in her forehead. He shrugs. "Because life is usually pretty stingy when it comes to handing out second chances." He's not sure if he has adequately answered the question or not. There's more that he wants to say, but his mind has become unhinged. He takes another swig from his Scotch and focuses on tangibles. He steps around her, walks over to close the front door, and then he stoops in the alcove to pick up the spilled library books and CDs.

"How did you know he had a baby?" Katie calls.

Lukas doesn't answer.

He's in the dark place. Back when he first felt the itch; back at the first place he was able to see the pain.

Chapter Twelve

There were hundreds of conversations taking place inside Longkesh Music Hall's auditorium, and Lukas could hear them all, individually, like the different instrument sections of an orchestra getting in tune before a symphony. The resulting sound was not harmonious, but it was energizing. It felt electric.

How nice you look, why has it been a whole year? We must get together this summer...

The girl is supposed to be quite good. I'm calling New York about her tonight...

This is about the time of year I usually plant the garden, but I just can't see the point, now that my Martha's passed...

The last boy is the one we're here to see. Yes, we've heard about him. We read the *Rolling Stone* article; I understand the fellow that wrote it is here tonight. Flew in just for the show...

Has it been an entire year? We must plan to get together when the weather warms up...

Lukas drew a deep drag from his cigarette, holding the warm smoke in his lungs while imagining the conversations the audience members must be having on the other side of the curtain. Sure, they would applaud politely for Jane, and for what's-his-name, but they were really here to see him. It was his party. And he was ready. As he stood with his back to the curtain, the expectant murmur of the crowd increasing in volume, Lukas didn't feel a trace of nervousness.

What he felt was more a sense of gratification, as if he had just put the finishing touches on a grand accomplishment. It was a rather paradoxical feeling to be experiencing, considering the curtain had yet to open for the evening, but such was the confidence Lukas had in himself. Tonight would be the first step. He was so sure of it, he felt as if it was already done.

He remembered a look that had impressed him, an expression that would occasionally appear on the face of one of the contestants of that television game show he would watch every day during lunch, a couple of years back. A contestant would know the category, but the actual question would not be revealed until they had decided upon a wager of a certain amount of the money they'd won so far. Once the wager was set, the host—Art Fleming?—would read them the question and they would have only a few seconds to come up with the correct response. But sometimes it was clear that the contestant had figured out the answer even before Fleming had finished reading the question. You could tell, because a unique smile would perch upon their lips—it was the same look, no matter who the contestant was. It was a look of achievement more than relief. Their faces would become portraits of sublime tranquility, as they'd politely wait for the entire question to be read, and then they'd respond with an answer they knew to be correct.

Lukas wondered if that same confident smile hung upon his own countenance at this moment. Tonight's question had yet to be asked, but Lukas was certain he'd already nailed it. He took another drag.

As he allowed the smoke to slowly escape through his nostrils, he felt a queer sensation, unlike anything he'd ever felt. A chill crept up his arms. He moved over to the piano bench, his head starting to swirl. A head rush? Lukas had been smoking cigarettes for almost two years now; filter or no filter—they were no longer capable of giving him a head rush. But he could feel an increasing pressure, as if someone were smothering his head with a huge feather pillow and gradually leaning into it with more and more weight.

Dropping his cigarette, Lukas greedily inhaled a deep breath, trying to blink the dizziness away. Was it the upcoming performance? Could his supreme confidence be betraying him, allowing doubt to sneak into his mind? Not a chance. Nervousness was a feeling that was completely foreign to Lukas. No matter how great the stakes, he was up for it. This feeling was something else entirely; his whole body tingled and shuddered.

Reaching to loosen his suddenly noose-like tie, he stopped, noticing a peculiar hum, like that of a far-away engine. Suddenly his vision began to cloud. His breathing quickened. Rapid, shallow breaths were all he could manage. Lukas had never experienced a blackout, but this was certainly beginning to feel like the way he'd heard it described. However, instead of fading to blackness, the familiar surroundings on the university's darkened stage began to be replaced by unidentifiable colors and swirling shapes. He thought he could detect a faint, musky smell, like polished vinyl. It reminded him of a furniture store, or perhaps the lobby of a car dealership.

Lukas could no longer hear the escalating din of the audience. His instincts told him to go find help, but he doubted his ability to walk, or even to navigate his way off the stage. He dropped onto the piano bench and tried to slow his breathing. The peculiar hum was growing louder. He could now recognize that it was a combination of several sounds. There was a tapping noise that sounded like a typewriter in some far-off room. Also, a familiar mechanical, swooshing rhythm.

Whoosh-whoosh. Whoosh-whoosh.

Lukas shot desperate glances in all directions, searching for the source of the strange sounds he heard. But it was useless. His eyes were not registering images that made any coherent sense. He was about to cry out for help, but he stopped, listening.

Whoosh-whoosh. Whoosh-whoosh.

The sound reminded Lukas of windshield wipers during a heavy rain. Since he'd been small, Lukas had loved to sit quietly during a car ride through the rain and think up melodies to accompany the swooshing rhythm of the windshield wipers in his mother's station wagon. He'd even caught himself doing it this very evening on the way from the restaurant to the performance hall.

Lukas imagined he could see the windshield wipers right now, dancing in front of him to the rhythm of the sound. Faintly at first, but they were becoming more distinct. And the tapping sound — it was heavy droplets of rain splattering against the car's roof and windshield.

The vision was coming into focus so clearly that Lukas could no longer see the hardwood floor he knew to be beneath him, or the towering crimson stage curtains he knew to be in front of him. He had been transported. All he could see were the wipers, struggling against pounding rain. The headlights trying to forge ahead into a stormy night — an eerie combination of fog and a heavy downpour that appeared out of nowhere to explode against the overmatched windshield. The dash board ... but this was not his mother's station wagon. He didn't recognize this car, nor the hands he could see tightly clutching the steering wheel.

Lukas rubbed his eyes, slapped his left cheek, but he could not make the vision go away. He watched the knuckles turn white as the hands tightened their grip on the wheel. Ahead through the windshield he could barely make out the outline of an approaching bridge. Incredibly, he could feel the car accelerate. It felt as if it was already travelling dangerously fast for such conditions. Faster, as if racing toward the bridge.

Then, in horror, Lukas watched the hands make an illogical — yet slow and deliberate — turn of the wheel.

Lukas was paralyzed. He could not reach out and grasp the wheel, nor could the driver hear his pleas. As he hurtled toward the guardrail on the bridge, Lukas found himself unable to scream!

Then it stopped.

Just like a stiff yawn will pop one's ears on an airplane, the pressure on Lukas's head was suddenly released and he found himself back on the dimly lit stage. Trembling, he stroked the back of his hand across his forehead and found it was drenched with sweat. His heart thumped so violently against his rib cage, it made him cough. His legs twitched involuntarily, and a sudden wave of nausea caused him to double over.

He wavered, supporting his weight with both hands on his knees, until the feeling subsided.

Lukas was gripped with uncertain relief, the sensation one experiences when awakening from a particularly horrifying nightmare. He tried to reassure himself that the terrifying vision hadn't really happened, but part of him remained unconvinced. His dreadful bewilderment was real, even if the vision wasn't. He blinked as he looked around the stage, unable to tell how much time had elapsed.

His gaze fell to the floor and he spotted his cigarette, still smoldering and darkening a tiny spot on the varnished floorboards of the stage. He straightened up and slid a shaky foot over to crush it out. Apparently the unsettling vision he'd just seen—a grueling experience that had seemed to take an hour to endure—had in fact lasted only for a few moments, yet now the stage was curiously silent.

Lukas endeavored to rise to his feet. Where had the audience gone? He shuffled on unsteady feet toward the stage curtain to have a look.

He drew back a sliver of the great curtain and stole a peek into the auditorium. What he saw filled him with a sort of terror he had never deemed possible. No longer able to support his full weight, his knees folded and he crumbled backwards, landing with a jarring thud on the oak floorboards.

Through the sliver of space between curtain and stage floor, his bewildered vision could see through to the other side of the crimson velvet. The scene had remained unchanged. The room was filled to capacity. Ladies were fanning themselves with their programs; gentlemen were engaged in unblushing conversations, punctuated by exaggerated hand gestures and laughter. Proud relatives were pointing out their children's names on the list of performers to anyone who would listen.

But Lukas Willow could *hear none of it*.

Lukas, who had never wasted a minute of his time doubting that he would one day take his place alongside the giants of jazz piano, had suddenly and inconceivably gone totally deaf.

Lukas used his palm as a suction over his left ear and desperately jabbed at his right with an index finger, not convinced it was possible. Surely he was still hallucinating! Finding his index finger too thick, he switched to his pinky and jammed it in his ear so far it made him wince. He sputtered, realizing that he had neglected to take a breath for almost a minute.

Furiously, Lukas clapped his hands. Nothing. Not a sound.

Lukas could now feel sweat—not drops, but sheets of it—cascading down his forehead, around his eyebrows, and down his cheeks. Panicked, he spun around.

The piano!

Lukas lunged across the floor towards it. On his knees, he flipped open the dust cover, raised two balled fists high above the keys and—

"No!"

Lukas stopped, holding his breath, hoping that he hadn't imagined it. It had been a woman's voice. Had it been inside his head?

"No," she said again, softer, but just as distinctly.

He could still hear.

Exhaling deeply, Lukas lay his sopping forehead down on the piano bench, ready to thank a God he had never spoken to. Instead, he abruptly imagined how ridiculous he must look. He shot to his feet, wiping sweat from his face as he turned toward the direction from which the voice had spoken.

But there was no one there.

Lukas peered into the shadowy wings of the stage, blotting moisture from his eyes with his tuxedo sleeve.

"No, no, no!" the voice cried.

Lukas frantically scanned the room. He rushed back to the curtain and pulled it aside, this time with a far less subtle touch.

"No," she lamented, her voice escalating. "It's all my fault! No, no, Jesus please no!"

Lukas's eyes darted in all directions at once, but he couldn't spot her. Some woman was quickly growing hysterical, yet no one in the complacent crowd out there seemed to be paying her any mind. Couldn't they hear her? Couldn't they see her pain? The woman's sobs were growing into wails.

The crimson curtain fell closed. Lukas felt a chill wrap itself around his damp body. He found it difficult to draw a breath.

He knew that voice. Worse, he somehow knew why she was crying. The bridge. It had something to do with the bridge. Invisible hands wrapped around his throat and began to squeeze.

Lukas looked down and noticed his feet were moving, carrying him. He was unable to control them. Out the stage doors, past the green room and the water fountains. A cluster of faculty members stopped their conversation to turn and watch him as he floated by. His stomach churned. He knew where his feet were taking him. The last place on earth he wanted to be.

The crying grew louder, more familiar. As he approached the ramp toward the reception area, the dread was gnawing furiously inside his stomach. He grasped for the railing, anything to hold onto, to keep him from moving closer, but it was no use.

A small group of people was hovering around Susan Collins, trying to console her. She noticed Lukas approaching, but no one else did. She was crying to him. And he knew why.

Don't you dare, Susan.

She reached out toward him, her grief and guilt lifting her quivering hands. He tried to back away, but he was pulled even closer. No one could see him but Susan.

Stop crying this instant!

Her hand reached for his shoulder. He wanted to pull away, but his muscles would not respond. He felt her hand fasten itself to his shoulder. To share the pain. Pain so extraordinary he could see it—from three rooms away.

It was time to reap the whirlwind.

***

All at once he twists free from her grip, falls sideways to the stone tile floor.

"Mister Willow?" It's Katie's hand, and her eyes are crying without tears. "Lukas?" she asks, "Are you alright?"

His body feels heavy, slumped on the floor of the alcove at the base of the stairway. He looks at the CD in his trembling hand, at the young man in the grainy black and white photo on the cover. So young, so confident, backwards on the bench, his back leaning against the keyboard. Cigarette dangling from an always-steady right hand, he looks off to the left, at something not present in the photograph. But something the young man had been certain soon would be present. *Dawn of the Rhythm*, by the Luke Willow Trio.

Lukas looks up at Katie's soft brown eyes, as if he'd never seen them, feeling feeble. "I didn't know they put it on CD," he says.

Katie crouches down beside him. "I got it out of the University Library a few days ago."

"Why?"

The lopsided grin coyly makes its cameo. "I guess I was interested in who you are."

Lukas looks at the fearless young man in black and white. "Who I used to be," he gently corrects her.

Katie unfolds her legs and sits on the floor next to the slumping man. "It's good," she says. "Really good. Nothing's in 4/4; I've never heard anything like it that worked so well." She sidles closer to him, and he doesn't draw away. He can feel her now-smoldering brown eyes on him, chasing him out of the dark place. Sweet Katie, unknowing. She could pronounce gravity a myth, and he'd believe her.

"You know, I've—I've been working on a piece—in case, well … in case I decide to audition," she says, her hands fidgeting. "It's in 9/8 time, and I've been playing it in sort of a 2-2-2-3 form, like you have on the second song on this CD. Except something's wrong with the transition; I can't seem to smooth it out." She hesitates, her shyness increasing. Clearing her throat, she continues, "Maybe you could listen sometime this weekend and tell me what you think."

Lukas runs a hand across his chest, over the folds of his belly, searching for a handle. He is certain there must be a knife sticking out somewhere. He shakes his head stiffly. "It's been too long," he whispers. "I don't know anything anymore."

"What happened?" she asks quietly. "Did it just leave you?"

Lukas is finding breathing arduous. He lays the CD face down on the scuffed stone, and slides it away from him. He shakes his head. "The music didn't leave me. I left it."

His words almost seem to echo in the sweltering silence that ensues.

"That's what I was afraid of," Katie says, swallowing hard. She rests back on her folded legs, placing her palms on her lap without a sound. She hesitates, as if clambering for words that her lips are unable to form. In a quiet voice she says, "I was afraid to ask, because I didn't want to hate you."

The words carry an electric shock. "Hate me?" Lukas sputters, suddenly defensive. "You don't even know me!" He shrinks back from her. "What gives you the right?"

Katie slides her hands up and down her legs, a delicate, nervous gesture. "I've been thinking about what you said the other day, when I told you I was thinking about quitting music." She shakes her head, and Lukas sees something in her deep brown eyes that wasn't there before. The familiar tingling starts to itch inside his skin.

"It's just not fair," she declares at length. She won't look at him. "There's too many of us, the ones who probably don't have it, who want nothing more than to walk away, but we can't. We tell ourselves that it's a childish dream, to forget about it and grow up, but we can't." The girl's words are toppling out of her, from a place deep inside where they've silently gestated and been rehearsed too many times. "We know the odds are a million to one, and we try to work up the bravery to admit to ourselves that we don't have it, that we're not one of the special ones. But we can't. We don't know why, but we just can't." Katie's eyes have drifted to that far-off place again. Her chin trembles. "And then there's you," she continues more softly, "and you definitely had it. You *were* one of the special ones. And still you walked away." She shakes her head. Her silence weighs down on her, bows her head. "It's just not fair. It's not fair to us. And … I guess that's what gives me the right." She swallows hard, as if steeling herself for his rebuttal, as a tear escapes her eye.

Lukas uses the door handle to help him to his feet. "I wish you'd go to bed," he says, and he stumbles toward the liquor cabinet.

Katie follows. "You didn't even play in the Senior Showcase," she says, and it makes him stop before he reaches the parlor.

"I looked up the old program in the library. You were scheduled to perform in 1981, but the reviews said you never went on that night. What happened? After that talk you gave me about how important it is, and you never even went on. Is that when you decided to walk away, right then and there?"

Lukas spins toward her, making her step back in retreat. *"Yes,"* he shouts. "That's when." He turns and stomps to the cabinet, retrieves his bottle of Glenlivet, doesn't stop to look for a glass.

Katie's voice subdues. "What happened?"

Too many questions. Lukas tilts the bottle back down from his lips, feels a cool drop of the liquor trace its way down his chin. She needs to stop asking questions. He doesn't want to answer. He doesn't want to bring her to the dark place. There are some places you can only go alone. He wants to erase the itch. He wants to be left alone.

He feels the glitter path warming his throat down into his chest. Her brown eyes are studying him. Those eyes. Lukas sees a beauty borne of pain. Sweet Katie, willing to sacrifice a love of music for a hopeless mother's conditional love. Lukas cannot muster the energy to maintain his anger. It seeps from him, like air slowly leaking from a balloon. Lukas feels a drop of Scotch slice a cool path down his fiery left cheek. It must be Scotch; it's been too long for him to recall what a teardrop feels like. When she said she hated him, it hurt, and even the normally reliable whiskey can't salve it.

He gives up. He drops to the sofa, sagging and weary. "The night of the Senior Showcase," he says, "My older brother was killed in a car accident on his way to the show. His car ran off a bridge."

His eyes blurry and useless, Lukas can't determine how Katie is reacting. Collapsed on the sofa, he cannot summon the strength to lift the bottle to his lips. He wishes for Katie's warmth beside him, and before the thought finishes forming, she is there.

A little more, a little further.

"It was foggy and rainy that night. The police said it was an accident. Stephen …" The sound of his brother's name spoken aloud smothers the night. Lukas closes his eyes. He wants so badly just to sleep. To disappear. His voice sounds choked and forced. "Stephen had just gotten married a month before. He'd just found out that day that his new bride had been … having an affair."

Lukas's trembling lips search for more words, but find none. The words have been missing for twenty years; it was foolish to think he'd somehow be able to find them tonight. Weakly opening his bloodshot eyes, he sees Katie's warm, red lips. Just her lips. Soft, dewy, and sorrowful. He feels depleted. He whispers, "I just didn't want to play the piano anymore."

Through the darkness, he feels Katie's tender breathing a few miles away beside him. She leans toward him. He tries to pull away, but she clutches both his shoulders. He is weak and she is strong. She silently kisses his burning forehead.

And the world explodes.

Part Two

Chapter Thirteen

Katie's eyes fall upon the envelope leaning against the base of the desk lamp, and she sighs. It has stoically occupied that spot on the desk for three days now, stamped and addressed, but Katie has been unable — or unwilling — to mail it. Stubborn maybe. A childish thirst for revenge.

The entire surface of the old pine desk has become a sort of makeshift shrine to postponement. A two-page application for entry into the Senior Showcase competition collects dust across its lines and boxes — all blank, save for Katie's name and student number. Next to it lies a stack of glossy, duotone pamphlets and other information on the university's nursing school program. Another student loan application, completed with black ink but un-mailed, rests on top of a battered gray folder that contains sheets and scraps of abandoned music — pieces of ideas that Katie has worked on but never perfected, like the unfinished thoughts of a distractible child.

Beneath the lamp, an old silver bracelet in desperate need of polish catches Katie's attention. It is the favorite piece of her rather meager jewelry collection, something she inherited from her grandmother. She used to wear it all the time, but a broken clasp has relegated it to its present spot on the altar of the neglected. Fixing or replacing the clasp is probably a simple procedure that almost any jewelry store could take care of, but Katie has never taken the time. She gently picks up the bracelet. She misses Grandma, how she would prattle around the apartment in Chicago complaining about the cold, making up silly songs to make Katie laugh, dispensing advice randomly and without provocation, just to get on Nora's nerves. Katie misses those uncomplicated days, how her grandmother would insure with such conviction that Katie's world would remain simplified, fiercely countering Nora's moodiness and cynicism with her constant assurances that everything would work out, and that Katie would grow up to be whatever she dreamed she'd be. Such were the luxuries of an elderly woman who knew that she would no longer be around when adulthood's rude entanglements began to reveal themselves. Although she couldn't have possibly predicted how soon after her death Katie's life would change so entirely.

For the past couple of weeks, Katie has felt trapped in a state of flux. The calendar suggests that she is midway through what was supposed to be the second-to-last semester of her college career, two weeks away from her twenty-second birthday. But Katie feels like she's attempting to move through time on a treadmill. Graduation has begun to loom larger on her personal horizon, but instead of approaching with a sense of relief or accomplishment, it seems rather to be accompanied by an entourage of doubt and apprehension. What was one supposed to do when they would soon be expected to take their place among the workforce, and yet the only means of earning a living they had ever prepared for or considered to be a possibility now seems like a dubious bet at best?

The prospect of pursuing a career that didn't involve music was one that Katie had never given serious consideration. Music had always seemed to be the obvious, natural trajectory that her life had been poised to follow. But now she is seven years old again, perched on her bicycle atop a hill that she has effortlessly descended dozens of times before, but this time the training wheels have been removed. Her safety no longer seems like such a foregone conclusion.

Each day Katie strolls along crowded campus sidewalks and passes increasingly unfamiliar faces. Gone are the comforting expressions on the faces of classmates with whom Katie had navigated through the perils of the early years of the undergrad music program. Competing good-naturedly for studio time during obscure late night hours, or popping up unexpectedly in the library like beacons of commiseration, they had seemed reassuring as they related similar stories of preparation for upcoming benchmarks, midterms, and finals. There had been a certain comfort in the shared focus on immediacy that Katie had been unaware of at the time. She has only noticed it recently, as those familiar expressions have been replaced by more seasoned looks of expectancy, as the issues and obstacles her classmates could now see coming into focus seem to exist far away from this time and place.

Yet Katie's horizon has not grown less blurry but more so, shrouded by doubt and a sense that she had been deluding herself all along when she thought she had been preparing for a feasible future. All of her self-righteous rejections of her mother's pragmatic and conservative intrusions—had it been mere adolescent rebellion? Trying to get back at her for what she'd done, or rather what she hadn't done? Could her mother have been right all along?

The break-in had rattled her far more than she had let on to anyone. The horrific feeling of helplessness, of being overpowered—it was like being eight years old all over again. It was as if the strong, independent young woman she'd spent years molding herself into had been destroyed in mere minutes. She wakes nightly, panicked from the nightmares that torment her. Not just of the stranger with the gun, but the old nightmares, the ones that had been leaving her alone for over a decade. It's like they had never been gone in the first place, as though they'd only been hiding in nearby shadows, waiting for the right moment to emerge and torture her again.

Perhaps she should have sought therapy all those years ago, like the guidance counselor at high school had once suggested. But Katie has always believed in solving her own problems, never been a big believer in shrinks. And of course her mother—who had steadfastly refused to believe Katie's version of what happened all along—had dismissed the notion immediately, decrying psychologists as quacks who prey on the emotionally weak.

So Katie, angry with herself for her weakness, has begun to spend more time away from campus, away from the synthetically-soundproofed walls of the studios, in the authentic silence of her tiny rented space inside Lukas Willow's home. She draws comfort from the quiet, peace from the isolation, even though part of her suspects that spending so much time at the scene of the crime may be hindering the healing process. But logic tells her that facing her fears head-on is the smartest way to eliminate them. And besides, Lukas's handling of the situation, although insanely unconventional, has resulted in her feeling comforted and safe in his presence. Overall she has begun to grow much fonder of Lukas, her initial mistrust—one which she holds for all men, to varying degrees—having begun to diminish even before the break-in. For a while she harbored a vague resentment toward him that stemmed from his past rebuttal of musical greatness, but that has waned as she has become more aware of an enigmatic sadness that seems to hover over him. He seems a kindred spirit.

Initially, Katie had noticed in Lukas a more legible reflection of herself. Although she had never consciously intended to do so, Katie realizes now that ever since the events of her eighth year she has been conditioning herself to seek a neutral outlook on life that would bubble-wrap her from the possibility of total devastation when things went wrong. It had seemed wise to aspire to gain such a balanced perspective, although an unavoidable byproduct would surely be the inability to glean total happiness or satisfaction from life's occasional blessings. Without lows, the highs cannot seem all that high. Katie hadn't thought of that. Not in time, anyway.

Lukas's incessant drinking seems to be his way of seeking a similar equilibrium in his life. Yet the melancholy that appears to accompany Lukas had from the start appeared to be more pronounced than any of the blues that had ever haunted Katie. Although he obviously tries to keep it hidden, something profoundly sorrowful lurks inside the man. It shows itself in the way his smiles evaporate so suddenly and completely. Not that he doesn't smile—she has seen him do so frequently and easily while sharing his company—but when his smile stops, it doesn't fade gradually the way most people's do, it stops with an eerily abrupt entirety, leaving only an impression of a close-kept sense of disappointment. It fascinates and confounds Katie. Surely the tragic and untimely death of a family member would be enough to throw anyone's carefully-arranged world into chaos, but to be devastated so thoroughly as to give up music forever? Something about it doesn't add up. She worries about him. When she had first moved in, she would see him almost daily in the parlor sipping Scotch in stoic solitude. And that had seemed odd, but in more of an eccentric way than in a sad one. But lately he has stayed mostly behind the closed door of his bedroom, and his absence from the parlor seems unsettling.

Most of the men Katie has known avoid showing much emotion, but Lukas seems like a decidedly extreme case. The night of the break-in, after they had talked, Katie had found herself caught up in affection for him, or possibly empathy. She's not sure. Whatever had inspired it, perhaps her kissing his forehead had been much farther over the line than she had realized. In the kitchen the following day, Katie had reached innocently for his arm in greeting, and he had pulled away. Lukas had tried to play it off, as if it were not deliberate, but the gesture had made Katie feel embarrassed and confused. Just when she thought she had begun to genuinely care about him, and that the feeling was mutual, she was forced to concede that she remained as baffled by the opposite gender as she had always been.

There have been numerous times in the past week when Katie has been on the verge of knocking on his bedroom door, urging him to talk, just to see if he is all right. But she has shied away from the notion, taking her cue from the fact that Lukas has never once ascended the staircase to her room. She takes this as a sign that her intuition of a friendship developing is premature. Lukas seems intent on maintaining a formal, landlord-renter relationship, and any attempt on her behalf to breech this invisible boundary might likely be considered an act of hostility. This saddens Katie. If she is to be lost in the woods of her life, it would have been pleasant to occasionally encounter a fellow traveler who had also lost his way.

Katie impatiently shakes her head, trying to shake off her gloom like excess water after stepping out of the shower. She is always disappointed in herself when she allows her neuroses to mire her in mental paralysis. Nightmares are just dreams, after all. The burglar hadn't harmed her. She is strong, and she has survived worse unscathed. She decides to take action. To force herself to snap out of this pitiful state of lethargic apathy.

She snatches the nursing information from the desk, decides to read through it. Almost as quickly, she decides she is not up to it at present, and drops it back in its place. To Katie, switching majors would be an epic metaphor for a person having given up on her dreams, and it's too early in the morning for metaphors. Instead she grabs the loan application and rereads it, inspecting it for accuracy. Finding it complete and correct, she decides to mail it without further delay. She looks at the nursing packet. The two are not necessarily related to one another, she reasons. Even if she were to stick to her original timetable, which meant graduating in the spring, her current finances would probably not hold out until then anyway. So the loan is necessary either way. Yet another loan. But at least she can put off thinking about nursing for another day or two, yet still mail a loan application and feel like she has accomplished something productive today.

Katie looks again at the envelope leaning against the base of the lamp. She decides to stop stalling and mail that one as well. Drop them both in the mailbox together. After all, there is no point in denying that these two are related. Sure, the loan will probably turn out to be necessary regardless of what she decides upon for next semester, but the check that sits folded inside the envelope leaning against the lamp removes all doubt. She looks at the neat and steady handwriting with which she has written her mother's P.O. Box address, trying to stifle feelings of indignation. She had left the envelope sitting idly for a few days, perhaps to allow her mother to stew a little, but there was never any doubt that eventually it would be mailed. Her mother's financial woes are self-inflicted, inarguably, but she remains flesh and blood, which means whether or not Katie will help her is not something that's optional.

Forgiveness has not come easy to Katie, but she forces herself to take the high road with her mother, to support her when she needs it, because that's what families do. Even though when Katie had gone through the worst ordeal of her life—at the hands of a sick man her mother had brought into their house—not only had her mother done nothing to stop it, she had refused to acknowledge that it had even happened ... which she still does to this day. Even with this extraordinary wedge existing in their relationship, Katie still finds herself on the giving rather than receiving end far too often.

It's not fair—her relationship with her mother—and it's an opposite dynamic from the way most of her contemporaries operate with their parents, but it's the way it is. Her mother is a taker, a leech, but Katie doesn't see herself as an enabler, or whatever the television psychologists are calling it these days. It's just that her sense of familial responsibility affords her no choice in the matter. Despite the resentment she feels toward her mother, she's compelled to help her when she's in need. In part, it's how she assures herself that she'll never turn into the kind of person her mother is. *Just keep doing what's right and you'll turn out right.* Helping a family member, no matter how despicable, is always the right thing to do. She is reminded of a line from Bruce Springsteen's *Nebraska* album: "A man turns his back on his family—he ain't no good." There it is.

Katie briefly considers pulling the battered vinyl record from her shelf and putting the song on, but decides against it. That would merely be another act of procrastination, disguised as motivation. Besides, she is hesitant to play music around the house when Lukas is home. He seems to prefer the quiet, and she doesn't wish to rack up any more points in the wrong column.

Instead she will walk down to the mailbox outside and post these two letters. It will be a physical act of progress, a symbolic gesture that she is fighting back against her own paralyzing indecision and paranoia.

She finishes sealing and stamping the loan application, then gets another idea. The bracelet. There is no good reason that she has not yet gotten it fixed. She sees it as a testament to her own laziness, or perhaps absentmindedness, or both. A small wooden stand is situated just outside of her room on the landing. If she places the bracelet on this stand, along with a post-it note that reads "Get fixed," then she will see it each time she arrives and departs from her room, thus increasing the probability that she will take actual steps to do something about it. In this manner Katie is able to fool herself into believing that writing reminders to herself to get something done equates to having done something.

She jots the post-it, grabs the bracelet and the two envelopes, slides into her shoes, proud of her self-motivated spirit, and yanks her bedroom door open. She is startled by the looming presence of Lukas, who stands at her doorway with timid knuckles raised in knocking position. His other unsteady hand cradles a steaming cup of tea. He appears to be more startled than she.

"Mister Willow," a dumbfounded Katie mutters.

He stands frozen for a moment, like someone who has just awoken while sleepwalking. He lets his knocking hand drop to his side. After another few seconds of awkward silence, he holds the tea out for Katie. She accepts it, and thanks him in a breathy, bewildered whisper.

Katie is too stunned by his sudden appearance to say anything more, or to take a sip of the tea. She wonders for a moment if he had been drinking the tea and had handed it to her merely as an improvised substitute for words he couldn't find, or if she had truly been the designated recipient he'd had in mind when he'd poured it.

Lukas is staring at the floor.

After another surreal moment of facing each other in stupefied silence, like two gunslingers that have forgotten how to duel, Lukas turns halfway toward the stairs and stops. Without looking back at her, he clears his throat and says, "I don't think you should quit music."

With that, he stiffly descends the stairs.

Katie watches him disappear into the hallway and thinks, What a very peculiar man.

Chapter Fourteen

Keeping one eye on the road, Lukas leans over to his right and fumbles through the glove compartment, feeling around for his sunglasses. With an unusually rainy autumn so far, It's been a long time since he's needed them. But today the sun is back, firing on all cylinders, glaring rudely in Lukas's face, as if to punish him for his complaints about all the recent rain.

He can't find the sunglasses, so he pulls the visor down and sits higher in his seat. Both hands clutching the steering wheel, Lukas takes a deep breath, lifting his shoulders with the effort, and exhales loudly, trying to will himself to shake loose of this depression that's been clamped onto him like a hiking backpack for over a week now. Lukas is aware of his gloomy personality by nature, but this has been getting just a little ridiculous lately. He decides to interpret this sunny morning as an omen, to take deliberate steps to craft a better mood for himself. If normal people can just "decide" to be in a good mood, then dammit, so can he.

Lukas is already driving below the speed limit, but he slows the car a bit more as his eyes examine the car's radio. He can't recall whether or not he's even turned the radio on since buying the car several years ago. Perhaps today is the day. The sun is out. He's tired of feeling lousy. Lukas punches the button. Maybe today will be the day that he'll be able to listen to music, like other people do. Maybe today will be the day that he'll hear a song and it will actually mean something to him, the way music used to, all those years ago.

Nothing but static.

Lukas presses one of the numbered buttons, then another. More static. It occurs to him that he's never programmed any of the buttons to receive a particular station. He turns a knob, looking for music, but the crackling white noise only grows louder. If that's the volume, how do you turn the dial? His fingers start to mash other buttons indiscriminately.

Finally, a button marked "SEEK" spins the numbers on the display and tunes in something other than static, although it is only a commercial for computer training classes. Not that much different from static. Lukas presses it again. More commercials. *Fall Sales Blowout! Hurry In!* Two more punches, and two more commercials. Lukas can feel a deep crease forming between his eyebrows. And not just from squinting into the obnoxiously bright sun, although that's part of it. No longer trying to hide or ignore his frustration, he slaps the radio off and scowls out at the world.

Coasting to a stop at the next intersection, Lukas shifts into park and leans his weight back into his seat. It's not the radio's fault. He stares straight ahead through the quiet neighborhood streets, knowing full well what's making him cross today. It's not the radio's failure to play a song that could cheer him up. And it's not the insolent sun, either. Two more blocks and he'll be turning onto his mother's street.

He doesn't want to see Gladys this morning. "Want" is probably the wrong word. It's been a long time since Lukas has been eager to go visit his mother. Nobody wants to be a witness to the rapid physical deterioration of their elderly parent, but that's not why you go. It's a responsibility, an obligation, just like a job, so you do it. Punch in, punch out. But today, even though he had only planned to stop by briefly before heading to work, it seems like more than Lukas can bear. He's already in a testy mood, so why add to it? And he certainly does not feel like running into Susan, either.

A minivan pulls up behind Lukas, and he winds down his window to motion them to go around him. He's got other obligations to attend to, after all. Lukas has been spending so much time with his mother lately that he's fallen behind at work. He never did fix that blasted sensor way up on the mountain. And now it's that time of month when Lukas is supposed to fill out the update reports and file the summaries of all the data that the sensors have collected in the past thirty days. Not to mention converting all the data to the Mercalli scale so he can forward his reports to the NEIC. He's got a lot to do. So if he just skipped his mother's house and went straight to work, it would simply be a case of a man trying to be a dependable employee, not a bad son. Welcome to Rationalization 101.

Lukas turns right at the stop sign and begins winding his way across town toward his little office. He's no longer facing directly into the sun, or perhaps it just doesn't bother him as much. As his mother's street recedes further behind him, Lukas feels a momentary sensation that almost seems like cheer.

He may not have the most vital occupation in the world, but a job is a job, and obligations need to be met. He should have fixed that malfunctioning sensor weeks ago. Every day, for the past week or so, it's been nagging at his mind. He's not sure why; the readings it takes are usually irrelevant or inaccurate anyway, thrown off by the incessant oil drilling on the other side of the mountain. But for some reason his conscience has been imploring him to get it fixed. He decides to pack a thermos tomorrow, make the hike, and fix the little bugger.

Today he will get started on all those reports, fill in some bogus information for the missing readings if need be, and get it all out of the way. Lukas nods, impressed with his diligence. His lips turn slightly at the edges, forming what could pass for a smile. He vows to complete all of the summaries by the end of the day, not like when he brought that stack of paperwork home two nights ago. He had intended to get a head start on the summaries and accomplish something in his down time, but all he had ended up accomplishing was the end of another bottle of Scotch.

Lukas makes another right turn and takes his foot off the gas. His smile sinks from his face. Probably the first step toward completing those reports would be to read over the data. The data in those files that he had brought home two nights ago. The ones that still sit untouched somewhere in his den.

Lukas veers the Volvo in a U-turn in the middle of the street and checks his watch. He'd left his house some fifteen minutes ago. He shakes his head. He is certainly starting off this morning as a virtual whirlwind of accomplishment.

***

Lukas flings the front door open, leaving his keys swinging from the lock, and is confronted by loud music. It stops him in his tracks. It's surreal, music being played out loud. In this house. His eyes climb the staircase. It sounds like folk music, or country, or some sort of garbage like that. Katie's door is open. The scratchy strumming of an acoustic guitar is descending from her bedroom, bounding awkwardly down the steps like a slinky. Lukas takes a step further into the alcove, reaches behind him and gently nudges the front door closed. *Does she always play music this loudly when I'm at work? And is it always this annoying?*

He briefly considers ascending the stairs, asking her to turn it down. Or at least to shut her bedroom door. He shakes his head; he's just being cranky. At least she has the decency not to play it when he's around. He'll just grab what he needs and leave.

He moves with rapid light steps toward the den, wary of letting his presence be known. He knows he's not being logical, but not only does he not want to hear Katie's music, he's even less inclined to be here if she steps out of her room. She would probably apologize for playing the music so loud. He doesn't want to have to endure an apology. Except for a brief and delirious moment a few days ago when he'd made her a cup of tea and actually climbed the stairs to her room—what had he been thinking?—he hasn't wanted to *see* Katie, let alone talk to her. She triggers the itch. Whatever's wrong with her, he wants to stay out of it.

He steps up to the counter and begins fishing through a disorderly pile of folders, magazines, catalogues and unopened mail. His hands are shaking. A gravelly voice has begun singing along with the acoustic guitar. Lukas stands still for a moment. The voice sounds familiar, like someone he should know. Someone from a long time ago. Lukas picks up an envelope, scrutinizes it for a second, and drops it in the nearby wastebasket.

Lukas hears another sound. Turns toward it. The shower? He looks up toward Katie's room, then back down the hallway. Is she playing that god-awful music while she's not even in her room? It would be just like Katie. Free-spirited, maybe.

Lukas turns and steps cautiously into the hallway to confirm. The bathroom door is open a crack. Steam escapes. She probably can't hear the music from in there, most likely wouldn't notice if he went up to her room and shut it off.

As Lukas considers it, he becomes aware that he has taken a few more steps in the direction of the bathroom. The sound of the running water grows louder. Without consciously trying to, he seems to be moving closer to the bathroom. And closer. He doesn't know why. Yes, he does.

He is only a foot or two away from where the bathroom door stands ajar. Through the crack, he can see the mirror above the sink is fogged over. He can make out indistinct shapes moving. He stares transfixed. He begins to take another cautious step forward, but catches himself in mid-stride. Immediately he averts his gaze to the hall carpet, shaking his head and scowling, silently cursing himself for his loathsome impulses.

He spins on his heel and storms back to the counter, begins thrashing through the mound of paperwork, knocking a folder to the floor and spilling its contents sideways across the hardwood.

The voice from upstairs sings about his brother, who *"ain't no good,"* and Lukas tries to ignore the irony.

His hands quivering violently, Lukas finds a folder he's looking for and tucks it under his left arm. His heart feels like it's banging against his ribs. The sound of the shower seems to grow louder, but Lukas refuses to look toward the hallway. More envelopes and papers fly to the floor. Scratches and pops now accompany the guitar. Lukas finds another of the folders he's looking for. Too many sounds. His head throbs.

Suddenly dizzy, Lukas grabs onto the counter with both hands to steady himself, allowing the folders pinned under his arm to tumble in an awkward flop to the floor. He closes his eyes, tries to calm his breathing and his haphazard heartbeat.

The singer mentions something about *"laughing and drinking."*

Lukas snaps his eyes open. Of course.

He turns and staggers across the den to his liquor cabinet. He snatches the closest bottle, unsteadily unscrews the cap. Brings the bottle to his lips as the bottle cap drops and disappears beneath the sofa. Lukas takes a deep swig, lets it sit in his mouth for a long moment before swallowing. Eyes closed, he exhales slowly. He can no longer hear the shower. His mind is beginning to calm. He can still hear the music, though.

"I catch him when he's straying, like any brother would."

Eyes still clenched shut, Lukas feels for the cabinet surface in front of him and places the bottle on it, taking care it sits upright. With all the concentration he can muster, he tries to will his pulse to slow down. He fears he's edging closer to some sort of mental breakdown.

"A man turns his back on his family, well he just ain't no good."

Lukas's eyes open. Damn.

He feels his shoulders sag. He slides the whiskey bottle away from him with a soft nudge. He turns in slow motion, crouching to scoop up the folders he'd dropped a few moments ago. He tip-toes across the alcove and out the front door without making a sound. Time to visit Gladys.

Chapter Fifteen

When Lukas appears in the doorway of his mother's bedroom, she doesn't seem to notice him. The sight of her gives Lukas pause. She seems to be lying more heavily, like she's sinking further into the soft contours of the blankets and quilts that cover her bed, as if at any moment she might submerge into them and disappear from sight completely. The bed itself is one of those adjustable ones you see advertised on television—Susan's idea—and at present it's propped up at a forty-five degree angle. Gladys half-sits, half-reclines, a picture frame resting on her lap between her withered hands, but her head is turned toward the window on the opposite side of the room from the doorway where Lukas stands. He follows her ardent gaze. The blinds are closed.

"Feel good to be back in your own room?" Lukas says, and the question is enough to fetch the old woman's attention away from the closed window blinds.

"Ah, hey kiddo," she says. "I didn't hear you come in." Her eyes look tired, and her face does not register the wrinkled smile that usually appears when he comes to see her.

The faint aroma of burnt tobacco that clings to everything in the room bothers Lukas. Coming closer, he recognizes the photograph on his mother's lap as the one of her and Lukas's father that usually hangs among the minions of other frames on the wall facing her bed. Lukas tenses. Attempting to stave off the mawkish conversation that Lukas suspects looms behind his mother's solemn expression, he interjects, "You should open those blinds, let some sun in. Nice day out there."

Gladys lowers her head, allows her eyes to drop to the photo on her lap. She says nothing. Lukas feels his pulse quicken. He hastens around the bed to the window. With his back to his mother, he tugs at the window blind. It takes him a couple of unsteady attempts, but he is able to draw up the blind. The room brightens by several shades. He squints out into the afternoon, delaying turning back around.

"You know what one of the nice things about getting old is?" Gladys says.

Here it comes anyway. Lukas swallows hard and turns to face her, readying his customary blank expression. "You mean there are some?"

Gladys is staring at the photograph, her head tilted to one side, the crinkled smile having returned to her lips. She maintains this pose for a long moment, until Lukas wonders if she remembers having asked him a question. As seconds pass in silence, Lukas feels his chest beginning to tighten. His mother seems to be off in another world, but Lukas's sense of propriety makes him hesitate, unsure what, if anything, he should say.

Finally, she speaks. "It's easier to let go of things." She smiles again. "A lot of people might think it gets harder, but it gets easier."

Lukas can't tell if she's talking to him, or just talking near him. Either way, it seems harmless enough. What is it that's making him so jumpy? He steals a quick glance at her bureau's mirror, just to assure himself that he's not visibly shaking.

Gladys taps a bony fingertip against the frame's glass, not as if she's pointing at it, but more an unconscious gesture—her body keeping itself busy while her mind is elsewhere. "When you're younger you tell yourself you have all these principles, these reasons to hold things against people. Somebody does you wrong, and you hold it against them, and you tell yourself you're right to do it. Righteous indignation. Hmmph." At least she tries to say 'hmmph,' but the effort makes her cough. The initial cough triggers more hacking, and then more, the intensity of which increases until Gladys is partly doubled-over with spasms.

Lukas doesn't know what to do. He moves to sit on the edge of her bed, scans the nightstand for a cup of water or something—anything. His heart races, lapping itself. He is sure something colossal is about to happen. He reaches toward his mother with a trembling hand, but just as suddenly as the coughing had started, it stops.

Gladys still holds a crumpled tissue to her mouth. She draws a couple of deep breaths—which sound more like laborious wheezes—and gives herself time to recover. Lukas crooks an eyebrow, sees himself, and bashfully drops his arm back down to his side, resting his twitching hand on his lap.

Swallowing a couple of times, emitting a smacking sound from her wetted lips, Gladys continues making her point, as if the coughing fit had been an expected part of the conversation, and she was glad to be done with it. "I think we hold each other to too high of a standard," she says. "Nobody's perfect, after all. So what's wrong with accepting imperfections, and even learning to love them?"

A tense Lukas remains perched on the edge of the bed, just out of his mother's reach. He is fairly certain now that she can see him shaking. He cannot maintain a steady gaze. He keeps glancing to different spots in the room, as if the mysterious dread he senses is lurking just out of sight. He is irritated by this elusive nervousness that taunts him but refuses to clarify itself, and also with his powerlessness to make it stop. He tries to shrug it off, to focus on what his mother is saying.

"Take your father, for example," Gladys says, in that soft tone she always adopts when she speaks about him. "He did plenty to harm me. He cheated on me, he lied to me, he frittered away whatever money we came up with, he *drank too much*." With this last pointed comment, she fixes her eyes at Lukas. He feels his face flush crimson. She's old, but not a lot manages to slip past her.

"But I loved him," she continues. "Still do, just the same as if he was sitting in that chair over there."

Lukas glances over at the chair in the corner of the room. He shivers.

"He did a lot of bad things," she says with a smile that belies the words she's speaking, "but that doesn't mean he was a bad person. He just did a lot of things without stopping to think how much it would hurt others. How much it would hurt me. He didn't do it on purpose. It was just a mistake, that's all."

Just a mistake. Lukas drops his eyes from hers. Now he knows she's talking to him. She may not even know it. She's just firing arrows into the air, dozens at a time, hoping one of them finds a mark. She always does this, and invariably it works. It's wretched, the way she operates.

"You know, I was mad at him for a long time. Years," she prattles on. "I had every right to be."

The folders in the car. The reports. Lukas isn't sure why they pop into his mind, but at this point he'll take any excuse to get out of here. Work. Obligations. He places his hands on his knees, ready to push off and begin his exit routine.

"Holding onto that anger didn't do any good," says the old woman. "Didn't hurt him one bit. All it did was made me miserable. Holding onto those hard feelings, it just kind of rots you out from the inside." Lukas can feel her stare, but he won't return it.

"Lord knows he didn't deserve to be forgiven. Even he'd tell you that. Maybe that's why forgiving him anyway made me feel so much better." She reaches for Lukas, but he doesn't budge. Remains out of reach. She returns her frail hand to rest once more on the photo. She turns to look back out the now-open window. "It's like I let go of all the bad feelings I had about him, let them float away, and I only held onto the good ones. And now those are the only ones I've got left."

As if it were that easy. Lukas shakes his head in benign outrage, and stands. His knees snap loudly as he straightens them. *Like they were little balloons, and you just let them float away.* He's preparing to explain that he must be going when he thinks about the reports in the car again. Something's not right. He can't seem to calm his breathing. He becomes aware of sweat on his forehead, wipes it off. She keeps it way too hot in this room.

"It's a shame I figured it out so close to the end," Gladys almost whispers. The smile has left her face. "I wasted a lot of valuable time along the way."

Lukas calculates that he's heard all he can bear. Clearing his throat, he says, "Well, I've got some important things to take care of at work today."

Gladys gives a slow, knowing nod, her voice now soft and low. "I know why you're upset. And I know—if we'd gone with your plan in the first place you wouldn't be in this position." Her face brightens. "I've asked Susan to pick up some of that pecan flavored ice cream you like so much, to try to make it up to you."

Lukas's mind races. "What are you talking about?"

Gladys studies his face for a moment before she responds. "Didn't Susan tell you about the conference?"

"What conference?"

Sighing, Gladys explains, "Susan has to go away for a couple of days, the week before Thanksgiving for some kind of nursing conference. Professional development, they call it. She's all worried about me being by myself, and she thinks I need someone to look in on me."

"Well, that's true. You do."

Gladys rolls her eyes and dismisses his statement with a wave of her hand. "Well, she was going to ask you to come by and check up on me. She didn't mention it?"

"No," Lukas says, replaying his earlier encounter with Susan in his head. He had strode through the dining room, straight to the staircase. They had only exchanged prim "good mornings." Maybe just nods. No talk about any conferences. The thought of being his mother's primary caregiver begins to tighten around Lukas's neck like a noose. He begins to point out that if she'd have let him hire a professional, they wouldn't be in this situation, but the words catch in his throat when he looks into her rueful eyes.

"I don't need you to baby-sit me, Luke," she says, her soft tone imploring, "but it would be nice to see you more often." She blushes, looks off to the side. "Look, I get up earlier than you do anyway. I could have coffee already made, and you could just pop in real quick on your way to work in the mornings."

This place is not on my way to work, he thinks but doesn't say. She smiles at him, a picture of hope. "I'll just do a little tap dance to show you I'm okay, and everyone will feel a lot better, and then we'll all go on with our business. It's only for three days."

Lukas feels his anger at Susan—at the situation—begin to ebb. For a moment, his mother is the jovial younger woman she was when he was small. The severe expression on his face softens. He shrugs, stuffs his hands in his pockets. "No, it's, it's fine … Mom." The last word feels oddly gauche as it escapes his lips. "I just wish she would have said something about it, that's all."

His mother turns to look intently out the window once more. "Well, she was probably afraid to say anything to you," she mutters. "The way you're so cold to her all the time."

Lukas winces.

"If you ask me," she continues, "there's entirely too many things that are left unsaid in this family."

This family.

Not enough things, if you ask me, Lukas thinks as he exits the room.

Chapter Sixteen

Stepping out onto the weathered red bricks of the courtyard, Katie blinks against the odd lighting that marks the gathering dusk. Bearing neither the hallmarks of afternoon nor evening, this time of day often displays a unique and surreal quality. Katie has just emerged from a free screening of *Cool Hand Luke* in Connolly Hall, and it takes her a moment to transition her awareness from the reel world back into the real world.

The queer sensation reminds Katie of similar experiences after having spent hours in the studio composing and rehearsing for various assignments and recitals. Invariably, Katie tends to get so completely absorbed into the alternate universe of her music that, afterwards, upon exiting the music hall basement, she finds herself needing a few moments to reacclimatize into the real world—to reassure herself that indeed that's what it is. As unsettling and curious as the feeling is, it's also rather wonderful, one that Katie treasures. Lately, one she misses.

"Latte?"

Katie turns. Her friend Sarah is re-wrapping a cashmere scarf around her neck and looking at Katie expectantly.

"Totally."

The two girls make a ninety-degree turn on the sidewalk and head for the coffee shop across the street from campus. Katie, finding new avenues of procrastination, had discovered an advertisement for the 5:00 showing of the classic film posted on a kiosk outside Longkesh Music Hall and had immediately decided to go. *Cool Hand Luke* is one of her favorite movies. Luke is tough, relentless, a survivor. Everything she strives to be. Sarah had agreed to accompany her after Katie had described various scenes featuring a young Paul Newman without his shirt.

Katie and Sarah had been roommates in the freshman dorm and have remained close ever since. They don't see each other as much anymore, as Sarah's MassCom major has rotated her into different campus circles than Katie's, but they only live a few blocks from one another and often meet up on weekends.

As they wait on the corner for the light to change, Sarah digs suddenly into her purse. Her cell phone is still vibrating as she retrieves it, and she flips it open in one smooth motion.

Katie rolls her eyes. Another text message. The crack cocaine of her generation. Katie's sensibilities had been highly offended by the frequency with which Sarah had sent and received text messages during the movie. During the movie! She was baffled by what could have been so important that it couldn't have waited until afterwards. It seems to

Katie that a certain etiquette exists during the performance of art that shouldn't be violated. Sure, the filmmakers hadn't been physically present in Connolly Hall while the images flickered across the screen, but sending text messages during a movie seems to Katie to be comparable to having a conversation during someone's piano recital. At one point she had been certain that George Kennedy had been glowering his disapproval at both of them from up on the screen. "It's her," Katie had wanted to explain, "not me!"

The light changes and the girls proceed through the crosswalk, Sarah expertly keying with one hand as she walks.

Of course the texting hadn't been nearly as annoying as the nail filing! *Ka-shink, ka-shink.* She had kept it up for nearly half the movie! Katie had never even heard stand-up comics talk about anyone filing their nails during a movie. *Unfathomable.*

Sarah tucks her phone away and opens the coffee shop's door for Katie. They exchange a smile. As they enter, the rich aromas present them a warm greeting.

"You look like you need an espresso," Sarah says, eyeing her friend. "You okay?"

Katie shrugs. "Just haven't been getting a lot of sleep lately."

"Oooh," Sarah's eyebrows lift in an expression of inquisitive conspiracy. "Do tell."

Katie grins. "No, not that. I wish." The girls take spots at the end of the line. "I've been, you know, having nightmares and stuff a lot lately. About the burglar." She hunches her shoulders, embarrassed. Sarah is the only friend to which she'll admit even the slightest traces of vulnerability.

Sarah cocks her head to the side. "The burglar?"

"I told you about that."

It takes Sarah a moment. "Oh, *right.* Yeah, that had to be hella scary! You should've called the cops, I don't care what your crazy landlord says."

"He's not crazy. He's sweet."

Sarah leans forward, looks at Katie out of the tops of her eyes. "Reiker, he's creepy."

"He is not."

"*Hannibal Lecter* creepy."

"Enough," Katie says, an exasperated smile on her face. "Let's change the subject."

Sarah's eyes widen. "Totally. What about next week? What's the b.d. plan?"

Katie shrugs. "Dunno. I hadn't really thought about it."

"Haven't really thought about it? Well it's time to start! This is a big one—the deuce deuce! No longer a freshman in the legitimate bar scene. A celebration is in order!"

"I guess."

Sarah spreads her fingers, pushing at the air in front of her, full of excitement. "Leave everything to me. Don't give it another thought!"

"Done," Katie says. They both laugh.

The line moves forward one step, in unison, like a marching band. "So what else is up, Reiker? We never talk anymore. What about Thanksgiving? Are you hanging out with your Mom?"

Katie snorts. "Hardly." She bobs her head from side to side thoughtfully. "I don't know. Maybe."

"Well, you're totally welcome to come back to Frisco with me. But apparently plane fare is none too cheap, according to my dad."

"Yeah, I don't think I could swing that."

"I swear. He can be such a cheapskate sometimes. He doesn't say anything, but it's like he gets this tone. And I'm like, W.T.F? Uh, you're the one who insists I come home for Thanksgiving. Hello?"

Katie smiles, imagining the farcical scene that would ensue if she ever even hinted at asking Nora to pay for something as expensive as a plane ticket.

"Have you picked your classes for next semester yet," Sarah asks, as they move to the on deck circle beside the counter.

"Umm, no, not yet. I gotta figure a couple of things out still."

"What's left to figure out?. I only have six more required credits. So guess what else I'm taking?" Sarah raises her voice and gestures in excitement, "Ballroom dancing."

Katie grins. "I don't know. I might end up sticking around a little longer, taking some other classes. I'm not sure."

Sarah studies her friend's face closely for a moment. Then she lightens and says, "Really? Nice," with a playful slap on Katie's shoulder. "We've got the rest of our lives to work for a living, right? Why stop the carnival so soon if you don't have to? I'm so jealous—my folks would shit egg rolls if I tried a stunt like that."

Before Katie can respond, the cashier asks to take their order and Sarah steps to the counter. Katie remains frozen in place for a moment, feeling peculiarly like a tourist trying to ask for directions in a language she doesn't speak.

Her mind jumps back to a moment during the movie when Sarah had whispered a comment that Katie now realizes has remained stuck in her consciousness. It had been during the scene where Luke and Dragline have their memorable boxing match in the prison yard. Luke is immediately overwhelmed by the bigger man's superior strength and skill, yet he keeps getting back up to doggedly continue the fight.

At some point during the bout, Sarah had leaned over to Katie and whispered, "Just like a guy—all muscle and balls, *no brain*."

Katie hadn't been able to nod, too dumfounded to respond. That's not what this scene is about, Katie had thought. Not even close! Strange how two people can look at the same sky, and one sees blue while the other sees red. The two of them had been sitting in seats side-by-side, sharing a common armrest, but there may as well have been three rows of empty seats between them. In the crowded, darkened theater, Katie had felt something that she might dimly have labeled as loneliness. Once again, she was the little girl in white.

Chapter Seventeen

Before he opens the drawer, Lukas visualizes what he will find within it. He is standing in front of the antique roll-top desk; one of the few relics that had already been in the house before he'd bought it that he'd actually kept. He had liked the look of it, the dark shade of wood stain and the faded luster of the varnish. However, he doesn't use it. Never sits at it. To his recollection, Lukas has never even opened the center drawer, so it doesn't make sense that he already knows what's in it. Yet somehow, he's sure it's in there.

Lukas pulls the rolling swivel chair out from the desk and lowers himself into it. Best to do these kinds of things sitting down.

Taking a deep breath, he reaches for the blackened brass handle and eases the drawer open. It opens without resistance, freely displaying the item Lukas had known it contained.

He cocks his head to the side, allowing himself to appreciate looking upon it for the first time. A faint smile nudges aside the somber frown that had hung upon his face.

Slowly, with reverence, Lukas grasps the handle and lifts the revolver out of the drawer. As if moving independently, his left hand delicately slides the drawer closed as he admires the weapon his right hand holds. The polished black steel of the barrel, the graceful curve of the handle. It's magnificent. He doesn't need to check to see if it's loaded. It is. He knows it is, and the knowledge fills him with such a delirious lightness that he feels he might float off the chair.

Raising the weapon, Lukas lets his eyes fall shut. He rests his elbow on the chair's arm and tilts his head to the right. The barrel's tip feels cool against his temple. He allows the full weight of his head to lean against it, and it feels more comfortable than any pillow he's ever known. It feels like falling asleep.

But just like the body will give a startling twitch during the first stages of falling asleep, a troubling thought flares in Lukas's mind, jerking him out of his reverie—his eyes snap open.

What if the gun hadn't been here when he'd moved in? What if it hadn't belonged to a previous owner?

What if it belongs to Katie?

"Luke?"

Her voice makes him jump. He spins around in the chair, and she is standing before him. She has just come from the bathroom, from the shower, and she is wearing only a faded pink towel. Lukas catches his breath at the sight of her.

The towel that she's wrapped around herself is damp, and its fabric, worn thin and malleable, clings tightly to the curves of her body. Water from her drenched hair, hanging in black strands, drips steadily onto her shoulders. Some of the droplets meander down the tender v-shape of her collarbone and find their way to the valley that forms at the center of her chest, where the shade of her skin lightens, before being absorbed into the frayed edge of the terry cloth. The towel's diminutive size is insufficient to modestly cover her nakedness, and she holds the towel in place at the spot where she's tucked it into itself over her heart, as if she fears that gravity alone might unfold it.

Mesmerized, Lukas allows his eyes to follow the curve of her hips, down to where the towel stops mid-thigh, well above the area where the gradual tan of her legs begins. Lukas watches as a single drop of water emerges from under the cover of the towel and traces a delicate path down the clean-shaven smoothness of her inner thigh and calf before finally finding its way to the stone floor of the alcove.

Lukas finds it difficult to breathe.

She is staring into his eyes with a noncommittal expression, almost as if she doesn't recognize him. He remembers the gun in his right hand and feels himself blanche. His mind scrambles for an explanation, but looking down he sees only his quivering outstretched hand. There is no gun.

Had he been hallucinating?

He looks back at Katie, an expression of plain astonishment on his face. He swallows hard. She is now standing with both arms at her sides. The towel sags a couple of inches, revealing the unblemished white skin of the tops of her breasts where the convex slope of her chest begins on either side of the slight shadow now showing between.

Lukas watches with unbridled fascination as the damp towel begins to slip under its own weight, and the spot where it's been tucked into itself begins to loosen. Katie draws a deep breath, and as her chest expands the fold works itself loose. The towel flops open and begins to fall, and Katie lets it. Lukas watches it slide off her body and drop to the floor. And when it lands in a heap, it makes the unmistakable sound of shattering glass.

Lukas blinks, staring at the crumpled towel. It had definitely sounded like glass breaking. He blinks again and again helplessly, the bewildered gesture of someone who's no longer sure the world is following the rules he'd assumed it must.

He looks at his own feet and notices shards of green tinted glass, and spots of hazy liquid splattered among them on the vinyl tiles of the floor.

His office floor.

That's where he is, and the swivel chair is the one that sits at his office desk. He looks beside him and sees it there, unchanged, and unimpressed by his wild and licentious delusions.

Lukas blows a loud breath out through his lips. He rubs both eyes with the bases of his sweaty palms and swivels back to face his desk. He forces his mind to refocus on what he was doing before the vision had overtaken him, tries to ignore the resentment he feels at not having had the will to prevent it.

He snatches the printout lying on top of the pile before him and looks it over. He flips the page, his eyes swiftly scanning columns of figures and jagged lines stretched across endless sets of graphs.

He drops the report back onto the desk in disgust.

Everything is completely normal.

All the readouts, all the data, everything in the reports—nothing even remotely out of the ordinary. Yet when he'd been sitting in his mother's room earlier, he had been certain that something was wrong. He had been seized with an unspecific dread that seemed so tangible at the moment, so authentic. It had felt like "the itch" had been trying to warn him about … nothing. He glances at the printers in the corner, humming away, the needles silently printing out what appear to be perfectly average seismographic readings.

Absolutely nothing.

Lukas feels a blackened ire beginning to ferment deep inside. Everyone complains from time to time that their mind is "playing tricks on them," but Lukas's situation is cruelly unique, and so is his anger toward it. He hates his mind. He's vexed by the way he is.

It's bad enough when he's able to sense things that most people can't, because the things he senses are always negative, always relentlessly depressing. But to be tormented by vague anxieties that hold no meaning or significance other than to fray his already haggard nerves—well, just how much was one person supposed to be able to bear?

Lukas leans back, the swivel chair creaking noisily with the posture. So this is what it's like to slowly lose your mind, he thinks. Not as romantic as the movies make it seem. Once again, fiction trumps reality.

He's troubled by the frequency with which Katie is now making uninvited appearances into his visions. There is something unjustifiable and unseemly, yet—he allows himself to admit—pleasurable about the way in which his subconscious seems to regard her. The way it seems to keep her stored neatly in the medicine cabinet of his mind, next to the other prescription drugs.

It's unfair, Lukas reasons, and it's not his fault. For whatever reason, he has been predisposed to be one of creation's freakish anomalies. His mind and his—whatever you would call the other thing—function independently, despite his misgivings or preferences, and he has no power over the whole operation. Just follow along sedately, like a homesick mule tethered to a westbound wagon train. Donkey, ass, choose your synonym.

But no. Before he can even finish lamenting that notion in his head, another part of his mind is suggesting that it's not true. Not entirely. It could be that his desire to leave his mother's room that morning was so strong that it forced him to conjure up an imaginary threat about the seismograph reports in order to provide him with a viable excuse to escape.

Lukas sighs. He grudgingly concedes that that explanation makes the most sense. It seems like just the kind of despicable thing he would do. Even his subconscious is depraved.

Lukas remembers the lyrics of the song he'd heard back at the house, and the memory deepens his scowl.

"A man turns his back on his family, he ain't no good."

He'll definitely go see her again, then; it's as simple as that. He'll leave work early. Maybe Susan will be gone by then. What a lousy day. The first time he's focused and *listened* to a song in years, and now it's going to haunt him for the rest of the day.

Lukas looks back at the broken whiskey bottle beside his chair and decides he'll make a quick stop at Chadwick's on the way to his mother's. Cliché, maybe. Or pathetic. But an ally is an ally. So it's settled. A quick stop at the liquor store, then back to Gladys's. It won't be pleasant, but doing the right thing seldom tends to be.

Lukas knows it's the right thing, because he has the whole situation filed, boxed, and organized in his head. The need to feel loved is instinctual. It's one of the few tools for survival with which human beings are armed upon entrance into this hostile planet. Well, normal humans anyway. Lukas understands this, acknowledges the responsibility he holds, his role in satisfying his mother's dependence on being loved, to whatever meager degree he's able. Or at least to keep up the illusion. His actions, half-hearted and disingenuous as they are, appear to work. The only measuring stick is Gladys's own perception. And so far as Lukas can tell, his frequent visits and clumsy care-giving efforts seem to be sufficiently pacifying the old woman's perpetual emotional exigency. So far as he can tell.

Lukas knows he's the outlier in this set of data—the rogue element that would leave the scientific experts scratching their heads. He cannot detect within himself any yearning to be loved. He believes it must not exist. Error Code 405: File Not Found. Gestures of kindness make him uneasy. Being shown affection unnerves him. Call it emotional claustrophobia. Another chapter in his unromantic descent into madness.

It's not normal, this feeling. Or rather, this conspicuous *lack* of a feeling that's supposed to be there. Lukas knows this. Doesn't understand why, nor does he strive to … not anymore. He merely accepts it. Perhaps the prerequisite need to feel loved is the result of a specific strand of DNA that he was somehow born without. Feeling-impaired. Not his fault, but a cruel twist of nature. He shouldn't feel guilty about his differentness; he should be given a special license plate.

Then again, perhaps the missing instinct is based on merit. The kind of thing where if one were to trample callously over the feelings of others, the ensuing punishment would be loss of ownership of said feeling for oneself. And this grim scenario is the one that makes the most sense to Lukas. Damn the inscrutable logic of it all.

Lukas's lips turn, but there is a smile that's missing, one that's somehow tied to those long ago dreams that have been forever maimed by life's cruel surprises and its distasteful sense of irony.

Grabbing two folders and carefully emptying their contents onto his already crowded desktop, Lukas stoops to use them as a dustpan to clean up the mess at his feet. He is so lost in his own misery that he doesn't even notice two of the needles on the seismograph in the corner make an erratic jump.

Chapter Eighteen

"We're gonna get *wasted*."

Katie can't help grinning at Sarah's unbridled exuberance, at the lilting emphasis she'd placed on the word 'wasted,' the pronunciation that made it come out a decibel or two louder and an octave higher than the rest of the sentence.

The girls are flopped on the front steps of Lukas's house, catching their breath after a short jog. There hadn't been much chitchat while running, but now the subject is turning to the plans Sarah has made for the evening to celebrate Katie's 22nd birthday. Clearly, it's what is foremost on Sarah's mind at the moment.

"What are you wearing," Sarah asks.

Katie takes another breath before answering. It's mid-November, and the cooler air has left a cramping in her chest that's not usually there after such mild exertion. "My blue and green blouse, I think. And jeans." She gulps water from a bottle they'd left on the porch.

Sarah's breathing does not appear to be the least bit labored. She's staring intently at Katie, as if listening to a surgeon giving a diagnosis of a critical patient. "The one with the frills around the collar?" Katie nods. Sarah seems to approve. "Nice," she says, then adds with a devilish emphasis, "That one shows off your *girls*." She winks, which is always a clumsy performance for Sarah. It usually ends up being more of a stuttering blink, and never fails to elicit an amused chuckle from Katie. "That guy Brendan is gonna be there. Have you met him? I think he's Sig Ep."

Katie shrugs. She finds it odd how Sarah tends to classify people according to what fraternity or sorority they belong to. There's a lot about Sarah that she finds odd, and it troubles her how much more frequently these things are coming to her attention than they used to. This is her best friend, after all.

"So I'll come by around six."

Katie blinks. "I thought you said eight."

"We're supposed to be there by eight. I'll come by at six to help you get ready. Unless that's a problem."

Katie is seized with guilt that her thoughts have been transparent. "No!" she blurts defensively. "Of course not, I love having you around!"

Sarah is obviously amused by this response. "Thanks," she says with exaggerated irony. "That's good to know." She rolls her eyes and gives Katie a playful shove. "Not you, *bimbo*. I meant will it be okay with your landlord? If I come by?"

Katie blushes. "O-ohh. No, I mean yeah, it's fine. Lukas won't care. You might not even meet him. He spends a lot of time in his room."

Sarah snatches the water bottle from Katie's hand. "Yikes, I'd hate to imagine doing what—"

"Oh stop. He's a really good guy. He's just...."

Katie's interrupted by the disembodied voice of Nelly Furtado singing about her promiscuous ways. Sarah produces her cell phone and looks it over. Katie hadn't realized that her friend had been carrying her phone while they were jogging, but it doesn't surprise her. The phone is like an extra appendage she's had surgically added to her anatomy. It mystifies Katie, wondering where she had been carrying it. Sarah's devotion to working out and obsessive scrutinizing of her diet have resulted in a taut body that would make swimsuit models jealous, and the minimalist attire she'd chosen for their afternoon run leaves no room for debate about that fact, let alone room for a cell phone. Katie can think of at least three nightgowns and even some underwear she owns that would be considered more modest than what her friend is currently wearing.

As Sarah's thumb furiously types a response to the text message she's just received, Katie shudders, remembering the frequent texts during the movie last week. In retrospect, Katie decides the vibrations—even when interrupting a movie—were far less irritating than the heavy bass and coquettish singing of Nelly Furtado that Katie must listen to with such aggravating frequency whenever Sarah is around.

Squinting at her phone, Sarah suddenly brightens. "Oh, for Thanksgiving. I thought she meant tonight," she says to no one in particular. She snaps the phone closed and looks back at Katie. "What did you decide about Thanksgiving break, by the way?"

"Oh, uh," Katie stammers, momentarily flustered to be thrust back into the conversation. "I'm gonna stick around here. I've got some music stuff I'm working on, and it's a good chance to score some extra studio time with most people gone for the break." She forms a crooked smile.

Sarah concedes with a perfunctory nod and then launches into a summary of the festivities she has planned for the evening. As she listens, Katie tries to radiate enthusiasm and keen interest, but in truth she's distracted by the pangs of jealousy she feels for the uncomplicated and whole-hearted way with which Sarah is always able to exist in the moment. MassCom majors don't have to worry about whether or not they'll be able to prepare an audition for the Senior Showcase Selection Committee. Or if they even want to. Katie envies people like Sarah who seem to have everything figured out.

Katie is looking forward to spending her birthday night with her friends, and maybe even getting a little crazy, but she realizes that tomorrow morning the things that are bothering her right now are still going to be there. The past will still be there, and it won't ever change, but the future is somehow even scarier. It's been far too long since she was able to fully enjoy anything, without something looming over her. Something complex to figure out, some important decision to make. If this is what being an adult is going to feel like, all the birthday parties in the world won't make the tradeoff worthwhile.

***

Lukas walks over to crouch in front of the cabinet to look for an old reference book he hasn't leafed through in years. He still can't shake the notion there's something he's missing, that the data's hiding something. Finding the volume he wants, he closes the cabinet door. As he rises, with stiff and ramshackle unfolding motions, he catches a glimpse of Katie and her friend perched on the front steps. Standing a couple of feet back from the window, Lukas lingers for a moment and watches them. From the back they look like full-grown women. But so often when he looks Katie in the eye, or when he sees her lopsided smile, she seems like anything but an adult. She seems uncertain and timid and altogether childlike. There's always something he wants to say to her, but he's not sure what. Too many important things end up forgotten.

Lukas has avoided her lately, and she has probably noticed that. Subtlety is not one of his gifts. She's staring down her own demons, of that much he's certain. Every time he gets within ten feet of her, the "itch" begins to torment him. Like standing too close to the fire alarm. But whatever her problem is, he's in no shape to try to help her. Someone whose torch has been extinguished should not presume to lead others along life's dark paths. Better to just stay away. Better for him at least, probably for her too. Small houses offer few options, so he's been spending more time in his room, behind his closed door. Away from her. Away from the itch. Away from the other feelings that he'll never admit to. Just forget about her.

She keeps finding her way into his thoughts, though. Too often. Pervasive Katie. But sometimes he won't even try to fight it. Sometimes the thought of her is the only way he can smile.

He watches her sit on the steps. Her hair is pulled high and tied in a disheveled ponytail. He can see the back of her slender neck, and one small freckle, and it makes him sad. He's not sure why.

Her companion stands and grabs her instep to stretch her leg. Lukas's eyes widen. This one's definitely a full-grown woman.

He looks back at Katie, and scolds himself. Katie has become a symbol to him, because she seems so innately pure. And good—like people used to be. Excessive isolation makes everything in life seem either symbolic or ironic, and a little less real. Lukas often finds himself daydreaming about a conversation they had shared in the parlor, or a particular look she'd given him, and thinking about how his reluctant smile seems not so shy when she's around. He'd never tell her these things. Not her, not anyone. It wouldn't be fair to her. Being a symbol is probably a lot of pressure.

He frowns, looking at the young ladies. Katie is, he reminds himself harshly, a real person, like all the rest. She exists. Not in his consciousness or in some abstract ideology, but as an actual young woman. Living and breathing. Not just a woman, but one from a generation that's entirely mysterious to him, one that's undoubtedly well-versed in the ways of cynicism and selfishness and tawdry betrayal and even, he dismally supposes, sex.

He tucks the book under his arm, turns on his heels, and heads back to his room. Away from her.

***

After stretching, Sarah says her cheerful goodbyes and turns to leave. Watching her graceful departure, Katie realizes she is also jealous of the way Sarah walks. It's more like she's flowing down the sidewalk. The bouncing pendulum swing of her blond ponytail, the gentle back-and-forth sway of her arms and the side-to-side sway of her hips, the undulating up-and-down bobbing of her prominent and perfectly round buttocks—all of her body parts working together in perfect, unthinking orchestration, like a symphony of movement.

And then she stumbles.

It is so abrupt, and seems so absurdly incongruous with what Katie had been thinking that she emits an involuntary syllable of laughter. Sarah doesn't fall; she quickly regains her balance and spins around to face Katie, a surprised yet amused smile beaming on her face. She gestures at a split-level crack in the sidewalk and calls out, "Tell your landlord I'm gonna sue!"

Katie pictures the comment as having "LOL" attached to it. Her smile tarries as she watches Sarah disappear around a corner. The fact that the crack in the cement had not been there a day ago does not register in Katie's mind. Instead, she becomes aware that—despite Sarah's irritating idiosyncrasies—she still maintains an abundance of genuine affection for her friend, and this revelation buoys her spirits.

Katie drains the last of the water in a great, thirsty swallow. When she turns to place the empty bottle on the porch behind her, she spots her phone lying beside the aluminum legs of a worn lawn chair. She picks it up and checks it.

No missed calls.

Katie places the phone on the step beside her and looks off to the western sky, where the sun has begun its slow descent from the pinnacle spot in the sky. It's almost three-thirty. Nora has probably forgotten about her birthday.

It wouldn't be the first time. Katie sighs. She's not devastated, not even indignant. She does feel a vague sense of having somehow been cheated. Not necessarily by her mother, but by life. Mostly, though, she thinks about Grandma.

Her grandmother passed away the summer before everything had changed. Before Nora had met Craig and invited him to move in. At first, Katie had been thrilled. Having never known her father, Craig had been the first substantial male presence in her life. She delighted in his attention. He helped her to begin to let go of Grandma. The old woman's absence had opened an enormous chasm in her life, a black hole in her universe that was too immense for her eight year old mind to comprehend. Nora had never been good at showing affection, at assuring Katie that she was loved and special, but Craig was. He bought her beautiful clothes, called her a princess, and tucked her in at night, just like Grandma had. She had looked forward to the late night tickling sessions with insane giddiness. Even after the first time he did the thing that hurt, Katie hadn't told him that it hurt because she was afraid he would stop coming in to tickle her. When their rendezvous began to consist of less tickling and more things that hurt, she didn't understand it. She just knew that it made her miss Grandma even more.

Other than the first couple of years after Grandma's death, Katie had never experienced loneliness with such intensity as she had during her time in college, and it has gotten worse with each passing year. She wonders if this is a normal part of growing up, or if she really is the anomaly she suspects she may be.

She had dimly imagined that Nora might forget her birthday, and she had challenged herself not to let it bother her. She has friends like Sarah, after all, who will share the day with her, and she will not be alone. Not technically, but—she admits to herself and to the crickets hiding beneath the porch—being forgotten by one's parent does have a way of making a person feel alone. It's unfair, the power a parent wields over their offspring. Katie wonders briefly whether she will even receive the obligatory card in the mail this year. It's usually a day or two late, and it's always signed the same way: *I love you, Mother*. It's a phrase her mother utters with relative frequency when they're together, but to Katie it always seems as if Nora is reading from a script.

Grandma, on the other hand, had rarely said it. Katie had not realized that until recently, and it seems odd. But perhaps she had not felt a need to say it. Katie had never doubted that the old woman loved her. The words weren't necessary. It had been obvious. Obvious in the way Grandma would never fail to drop what she was doing to spend time with Katie whenever she approached. How Katie had felt completely at ease telling her grandmother anything—a comfortableness that she had never felt with her mother. How Grandma intuitively seemed to know when Katie needed cheering up and would appear and place a pacifying hand on her shoulder. Or sporadically break into song—silly, nonsensical little made-up verses about Katie's specialness. How had Nora managed not to inherit these parenting instincts?

Katie feels her eyes welling. She draws a deep breath and exhales sharply, trying to force the tightness from her chest. The neighbor's collie goes trotting past on the sidewalk without looking in her direction. All at once Katie wishes it wasn't her birthday. She looks down at her arms and legs to make sure she's not disappearing. She cannot dislodge the impulse to cry, yet no tears come.

She's startled by movement to her right.

Lukas is standing at the top of the stairs, staring off into the opposite direction.

"M-mister W-willow," she says, smitten with unspecific embarrassment. "I—I didn't r-realize you were home." Turning away from him, she brings a fluttering hand to her face, but there are still no tears to wipe away.

"Hi," is all he says, and he says it in a manner that is singular and strange, even for him. For an arrested moment, Katie is filled with panic, her mind racing to recall what she and Sarah had said about him that he may have overheard.

He sits. Not beside her, but near her, a step above her and about three feet away. Seconds pass, and the bulky silence grows gigantic. She faces straight ahead, afraid to look at him, caught in an awkward transition between loneliness and self-consciousness. Before she can settle into one of the two categories, she's distracted by a quiet scraping sound. She looks over and sees Lukas sliding a small gray cardboard box toward her. She blinks, not comprehending the action.

Lukas's stare remains transfixed in front of him, his brow furrowed as if he's concentrating on something. The right half of his mouth twitches a couple of times, and then he clears his throat. "I'm not sure if … if it counts, as a—a birthday present," he says. Still he does not look at her.

Katie feels her jaw fall open a few inches. She stares at the box, uncertain and at a loss to guess how he possibly could have known about her birthday. All traces of loneliness and embarrassment have been displaced for the moment by utter and complete shock.

She picks up the box and lifts off the lid. In it lies her grandmother's bracelet, polished and affixed with a new clasp.

Slowly, Katie lifts her eyes to look at Lukas. Half his mouth arcs slightly upward, but she wouldn't call it a smile. Creases still mark his forehead, and his gaze is still pointed straight ahead. He says in a faltering, subdued voice, "There's a jewelry store on the same block as my office. I saw your note that you wanted to get it fixed." A pause. "I figured it was on my way."

Time stops passing, and the moment hangs suspended in the silent afternoon air. Katie turns and stares back out at the western horizon. This time she makes no attempt to wipe away the tear that traces silently down her cheek.

Chapter Nineteen

The dog's barking is frantic, relentless. Lukas can't see it, but its yelping is impossible to ignore. It detracts from everything else. The mongrel's probably straining at a leash somewhere close by, trying to lunge at a passing squirrel, but it's carrying on as if the universe is collapsing in shattered pieces around it.

Lukas resents the animal's lack of manners, its audacity to interrupt such a genteel and elegant affair, and he's sure those around him share his sense of being affronted. He wonders what sort of oafish, irresponsible owner would allow his pet to continue such uncivil behavior.

He tries to put the barking out of his mind and focus on the Christmas tree. It's elaborately yet tastefully decorated, and its sheer enormousness is impossible to overstate. Lukas marvels that they were able to somehow squeeze it inside the building. It's been positioned under the dome, the only ceiling Lukas can recall in town that's higher than the massive tree itself.

The auditorium's lights dim, and a hush falls over everyone except the insolent dog outside. As the tree's lights are illuminated by the turning of an unseen switch, the assembled crowd catches its collective breath, awed by the majesty of the display. After a moment of silent appreciation, a smattering of clapping erupts that quickly swells into a thunderous ovation. The assembly has risen to its feet for the lighting, and the volume of the ensuing applause finally drowns out the dog's barking. Indeed, the rousing outpouring of enthusiasm feels as though it's shaking the very foundation of the room.

Lukas's hands involuntarily stop in mid-clap.

He looks down at his feet. It feels as if he's standing on a floating barge rather than on solid ground. It's not his imagination. The room *is* trembling. Gradually others begin to notice, and the cheering starts to diminish. Eyes turn toward his, and he perceives a faint hint of accusation in them.

In an instant the applause evaporates altogether, and once again the frenzied barking can be heard, joined now by a low rumbling sound, distant and menacing. The shaking grows more pronounced. People grab onto the backs of chairs to steady themselves, their eyes wide with unabashed fear. The giant Christmas tree sways and shivers. People begin to scramble over and around seats in an ungraceful exodus toward the doors.

Lukas stands frozen in place, waiting to wake up. Surely this must be another cruel dream. Ornaments quake and flitter off the tree, shattering on the floor. A window to his left cracks. The frightened murmur of the crowd escalates to a panicked din. The tree's lights flicker as it starts to teeter dangerously to one side. A window near the exit explodes, and a few terrified people shriek under cascading shards of glass.

Bits of plaster are falling across the room like deformed snowflakes. Lukas watches in horror as the gigantic tree slowly succumbs to gravity and pitches forward. People scurry to get out of the way, but not everyone can. Its lights go out as it lands in a nauseating heap of cracking timbers and bones. The room is cast into immediate and total darkness.

The rumbling and desperate screams swell, combining into a deafening roar.

A few emergency lights snap on near the exits, but their faint light only casts an eerie pallor across the chaotic jumble of humanity as people struggle to maintain balance and make their way to the exits. A small boy huddles beneath a chair, wailing for his mother. Larger pieces of debris fall, entire pieces of the dome. Lukas is thrown sideways. He lands in a floundering heap in a chair. He is unable to move. In a paralyzed stupor, he watches the surreal hysteria of the scene unfold.

Lukas hears a different sound now, an unnatural and sickening cracking noise like the collapse of a giant redwood. Looking up, he strains his eyes against the thickening dust and the darkness. He can barely make out what appears to be a colossal dark shape, and it's growing larger. Whatever it is, it's hurtling toward him like an enormous bomb dropped from the heavens.

Only a fraction of a second before it lands, Lukas recognizes it as the University's pride—the ancient copper bell, broken free from its tower. And then all is silent, and there's only blackness.

***

Lukas awakens, coughing and choking. He has not been crushed beneath the immense artifact, but he's not sure where he is.

He can still feel the room quaking, but after a moment he realizes it's not the room. He is the one that's shaking. He pushes himself into a sitting position and scans his darkened surroundings. He decides that he's in his own bedroom. He runs his hand across the sheet beside him. He's shocked to find it's saturated, as if someone had dumped a bucket of water over his bed. His clothes, his hair—everything is completely soaked. It doesn't seem possible that one person could secrete such a profuse amount of sweat.

He swings his legs out from under the sopping sheet and sits on the edge of the bed with his head in his hands. He tries to calm his breathing and the violent shuddering coursing through his body.

He's as furious as he is frightened. It's the third time in as many weeks that he's had to endure this same nightmare. Every grisly detail, every agonizing moment are the same each time. He resents having to go through it, and he's angry that he can't make any sense of it. At first he'd assumed it to be tied to the persistent foreboding he'd been feeling while he was awake these past few weeks. The itch seems determined to convince him that something is wrong, but he has checked and rechecked every reference book he can find and every piece of data he's collected, and—except for a single irregular printout a few days ago—he can find no confirmation of anything out of the ordinary happening beneath the earth's surface. Still, the notion haunts him.

It's the peculiar setting of the nightmare that perplexes him. Obviously it takes place in the Longkesh Music Hall auditorium; that much he recognizes. But he's been unable to define the connection to Christmas. The University's student council annually decorates a pine tree, and they tend to make a ceremony out of lighting it, but traditionally they choose the tallest of the pine trees that grow naturally on the east lawn. They would never even consider cutting down a live tree just to decorate it—the University's reputation for being environmentally progressive makes such a notion unthinkable. There has never been an occasion where they've had an indoor tree, nor would it be structurally possible to fit such a large tree through any of the auditorium's doorways. The fictional tree in the nightmare must instead be some sort of symbol for the Christmas season itself. Lukas is getting sick of symbols.

It could be that the itch is trying to warn him that an earthquake will happen sometime during the holiday season. But if that's all there is to it, why is there no data to verify the possibility? And why does the dream contain all the vivid and particular details? Lukas has experienced clairvoyant visions before, but never have they been so specific, and never have they repeated themselves with such gruesome accuracy.

More likely it's a case of his subconscious randomly tying the holiday season together with the threat of an earthquake for no other reason than the fact that Lukas dreads both of them. A fear cocktail. Lukas views the Christmas season with the same apprehension that others hold for public speaking engagements or tax audits. The sentimentality, the cheerful façades, the traditions and familial obligations—it's like an approaching death sentence. Even worse, this year the festivities are sure to include Susan; that much seems unavoidable. The garnish on the fear cocktail.

Lukas sits for several moments in glum rumination, unable to rid his thoughts of the abhorrent images from the nightmare. His nerves gradually calm, but his resentment grows. He is tired of being a prisoner. Tired of being subjected to this torture, over and over, with no end in sight. Lukas tries to draw consolation by reminding himself that when the time and the circumstances are right, he'll be able to stop the madness—to outwit the itch, his dreams, and destiny once and for all.

But the right time and circumstances—Lukas prefers to think about it in these subtle and proper terms—are probably still distant on the horizon. In the meantime, there's no chance he will be able to go back to sleep. He glances at the clock on his nightstand. 10:24. It's still early. He has time to get to the liquor store before it closes. He stands and peels off the t-shirt that's plastered to his chest. The itch is not going to get the best of him tonight, dammit. The best defense is a good offense. It's time to get going.

***

By the time he pulls into the parking lot of Chadwick's, Lukas's mood has lightened. His mother will not live forever, after all, so he won't have to either. Eventually his shift will end, and he'll be able to clock out. Also, logic has convinced him that the harrowing incubus had not been a premonition at all. Just a bad dream. Attaching too much significance to it would be pointless and self-defeating.

He has recalled something Katie had said once about nightmares: "It's better to face them at night than during the day. At least at night you can wake up from them." Classic Katie. An off-handed remark. She probably doesn't realize how much wisdom she possesses. The accidental philosopher—too young to realize she's too young to be so wise.

Lukas feels a smile attempting to form on his lips as he enters the store. Thinking about Katie tends to do that. The door's bell jingling behind him, he makes his way down the familiar aisles and decides to treat himself to a top-shelf bottle of Macallan.

Striding up to the counter, Lukas considers how inappropriate it would seem to people if they knew how he manufactures hope for himself. So synthetic, and even morbid. But inwardly he shrugs, and his half-smile endures. Things are the way they are.

The cashier rings him up and slides the narrow, upstanding paper bag toward him. "You have a nice night, Mister Willow," he says.

Lukas looks up at him briefly. He grabs the bag and manages a genuine, full-fledged smile. "You too, Jake."

Perhaps his uncharacteristically cheerful mood causes Lukas to pull open the door with more force than necessary, but whatever the reason, the motion causes the tiny brass bell above the exit to come loose from its base. It lands at Lukas's feet with a stifled clink.

Lukas swallows hard and steps over it, back into the expansive night. He's sick of symbols.

Chapter Twenty

As Katie reaches the exit, she scans the bar for Sarah, to double-check that her friend is aware that she's leaving. They had just discussed the possibility a few minutes ago in the rest room, but Katie's mind is swirling from one or two Cosmopolitans too many, and she wants to be certain.

She spots Sarah on the nearby edge of the tiny dance floor giving her two enthusiastic thumbs up, and she grins in return.

"Ready?" Brendan says with an entreating smile, one hand on the door handle, ready to open it for her.

Allowing her heavy eyelids to fall slightly, Katie takes his arm. As they step through the door onto the sidewalk, she can hear the music pause and a bartender bellow, "Last call!"

The chilly night air catches Katie off-guard and she shivers, lacing both her arms through one of Brendan's and holding him closer. She nuzzles her cheek against his shoulder and breathes in the wonderful scent of his cologne. They cross the street and stop under a streetlight. Brendan turns her to face him and slips his arms around her waist. "You cold?" he says, grinning down at her.

Katie shivers with exaggerated vigor in his arms, and says with a deadpan, "No … why d-d-do you ask?"

He smiles wider and rolls his eyes, tossing his head back with the motion. "You want my sweatshirt?"

"I'm okay," she says, placing her palms on his chest.

"You want my pants?"

She snorts, feels her grin spread. Rolling her eyes, she says, "Nice…"

When he smiles, he keeps his lips closed, and he tends to accentuate the gesture with a lot of movement of his eyebrows. Katie finds it charming and undeniably cute, yet it reminds her of some movie star that she can't pinpoint. She briefly wonders if Brendan has spent time in front of a mirror, practicing his facial expressions in an effort to maximize his allure. The absurd image she conjures makes her giggle.

"What?"

Katie shakes her head. "Nothing," she replies tenderly. Inclining her head slightly forward, she looks up at him out of the tops of her eyes. Ordinarily Katie doesn't go for guys who are much larger or taller than she is, but birthday celebrations and copious amounts of alcohol have a way of letting the air out of old fears.

He leans toward her and kisses her. His lips are warm and soft; they send another shiver down her back. She pulls him closer. She is certain her mouth must taste like stale lemon drops, but he doesn't seem to mind. She explores his mouth with her tongue, and tugs gently on his lower lip with her teeth as he draws back to look at her.

"Wow," he whispers.

"Mmmm." Their bodies are pressed close together, and she can feel a slight pressure begin to press against her waist. She knows he's as genuinely impressed as he says he is.

"So, happy birthday," he says.

She smiles again. "Let's walk," she says, pulling him along. "It's freezing." She doesn't want to think about her birthday.

They walk in silence down the block, until the muffled music from the bar grows imperceptible. Her legs feel wobbly. From the alcohol, probably, but also because she hasn't kissed anyone in several months. She licks her lips; she can still taste him, can still feel a little tingle where her lower lip had scraped against the stubble on his.

They stop at the next corner under some low hanging branches that block the street's lights. It's too dark to see his face. This unnerves her, but she forces herself to imagine that one of his irrepressible smiles is arranged upon it. He pulls her close to him, sliding his hands down to pause for a moment on her waist, then inching lower and coming to rest at the tops of the back pockets of her jeans. His hands are warm, and she likes them there. She's okay, she's still in control.

They kiss again, longer this time, cloaked in the night's darkness. This time, instead of being able to enjoy the soft wetness of his kiss, Katie finds her attention invaded by random and discordant thoughts. No phone call from Nora. Music. Nursing. The burglar. Craig. Lukas.

Brendan pulls back, his lips only centimeters from hers. "My car is about a half a block that way." He gives her butt a playful squeeze.

Katie resents having her good time interrupted by un-beckoned and unwelcome thoughts. She grabs Brendan and kisses him hard, trying to banish them from her mind. Their tongues work furiously. He runs his hands up the front of her shirt, finding her heaving breasts. She tries to concentrate on how good his cold fingertips feel through the sheer cups of her bra, as her nipples begin to grow rigid.

But it's no use.

She pulls back. It's too dark.

"What's wrong," Brendan asks, out of breath.

"I don't know." She sighs, backing out from under the shadows of the branches.

Brendan follows her. "Let's go to my car."

She hesitates a moment. Her glorious alcohol buzz has abandoned her. "My house is just down this street a couple of blocks," she says, her voice tinged with disappointment.

"Yeah, but my car's right here. Let's go back to my place for a little while. Have a nightcap."

Katie remains silent for a moment. She doesn't want to disappoint him. He's sweet. She wishes she could make him understand, but she can't find the right words. How can you explain to someone that you can't make out with them because you're too distracted by glitches in your life's software? It would sound crazy.

"What's the matter?" Brendan persists. "What are you thinking about?"

Katie says nothing.

"Sarah's right. You seem distracted by something; you have all night. What's on your mind?"

Sarah would probably be naked with this guy by now, having a great time. So what's wrong with me? "I – I … I don't know. I'm just—just not sure … about a lot of things." She gropes for the right things to say, but they stubbornly elude her.

"You're not sure about me," Brendan says, pulling her toward him again. Too hard this time. Her heartbeat gathers speed. "That's normal. You never know if something's gonna be right or not. You don't know how it'll turn out." She can see him tilt his head to one side as she gently frees herself from his grasp. He's probably trying to read her expression, but hopefully it's too dark. "What's wrong?" he says, clearly disappointed that she backed out of his embrace.

"Nothing," she says quickly, embarrassed.

He sighs. "Look, if it seems like it could be right," he continues more softly, "then why not try it? What's the worst that could happen—you turn out to be wrong? Well hell, there are worse things in life than being wrong."

Katie blinks. That's it. As if a light switch has just been flipped on, clarity returns. It seems so simple.

"You're right," she says, shocked to realize that it's true. "You're absolutely right."

She grabs his face with both hands and kisses him. Hard, but briefly. She steps back and turns to walk toward her house. "Call me tomorrow, okay?" she calls back to him. "And thanks for understanding."

Brendan stands immobile at the edge of the shadows, mired in such stunned confusion that he's unable to answer her as he watches her disappear into the next set of shadows.

Chapter Twenty-One

The dining room smells old.

Its furnishings sit in adamant refusal to admit they've been abandoned, unwilling to own up to their ultimate irrelevance. A candelabra-style chandelier hangs suspended above a table that's covered by faded varnish, a graying lace tablecloth, and a hardy layer of dust. A full-sized china cabinet, also dusty, that now appears as antiquated as its porcelain contents, looms behind the table. An oddly enormous deep freezer, long since unplugged and silenced, sits in one corner, buried beneath stacks of cookbooks and magazines and a random assortment of irregularly shaped kitchen devices and serving dishes. The whole scene reminds Lukas of one of those rooms in a museum that have been cordoned off from visitors and painstakingly decorated with relics from a bygone era.

Lukas judges that it's been over a decade since anyone has sat down to dine at this table. He surveys the room again, this time noticing the wispy cobwebs clinging to each arm of the chandelier. Cleaning this room will require great effort, and Lukas thoroughly regrets having agreed to do so. His wandering gaze pauses on the china cabinet. Undoubtedly Gladys will want to use her mother's china for the meal, and undoubtedly it will all need to be washed before it's useable. And of course there is no automatic dishwasher in this house. Lukas scans the stacks of plates and saucers, imagining the thick film and dust that surely coat them by now. His eyes stop when he spots two identical children's mugs sitting beside some stemware, one emblazoned in gold lettering with the letter L, the other with an S. Lukas swallows, but his expression does not change. After a while, you get used to seeing things you don't like.

The dining room has two entrances, and Lukas stands brooding in the one leading to the kitchen. He looks over at the other doorway, the one that leads to the living room, as he hears the familiar clinking and shuffling of his mother's walker coming from that direction. It's an altogether unpleasant combination of sounds, reminiscent of the tortured gait of Jacob Marley as he lugged his damning chains with him through eternity. Seeing his mother propped up in bed, as is the case during many of Lukas's visits, is miserable enough, but watching her hobble feebly around the house with her walker is even less bearable. Lukas's mind flickers briefly to the emergency stash he has brought with him to the house—two fresh bottles of Scotch, safely tucked away in his duffel bag.

After what feels like an incomprehensibly long delay, Gladys appears in the doorway to his left, leaning heavily against her walker and breathing hard from the exertion. The Ghost of Thanksgiving Past.

She looks at him expectantly. "Well," she says, "what do you think?"

Lukas, humorless, feigns a grin. "I think I ought to go buy some velvet rope and charge admission."

Gladys sputters short, breathy sounds of laughter. For a moment, Lukas thinks she's about to have another coughing fit, but she recovers and says, "Yeah, I s'pose saying that this room has fallen into neglect would be putting it lightly." She pauses, as if waiting for Lukas to respond. He doesn't.

She makes her way gingerly to one of the stiff wooden chairs arranged around the table. Lukas steps forward to pull it out for her, but she waves him off. She plops down into it and spreads her withered hands across the lace patterns of the tablecloth. "Oh, it'll be so nice," she says, a disjoined smile hovering on her face. "A good old-fashioned holiday feast, just like the old days."

Lukas frowns, yet maintains silence, unwilling to point out the obvious. Their conversation the night before had been a long and tense negotiation, before Lukas had finally relented and agreed to the "traditional" Thanksgiving dinner. He still shudders at the thought, but he keeps his peace, not wishing to stir up any more unpleasantness.

As if reading his thoughts, Gladys says, "I know you think it's silly, but just content yourself with knowing you're making an old woman happy. You get points with the angels for things like that, you know." She winks.

Lukas presses his lips together tightly in the expression he has come to use over the years as a substitute for a smile. Inwardly he scoffs. The old woman might still outlive them all, he thinks helplessly. He's not entirely convinced that it's angels who are protecting her.

Gladys fumbles through her sweater pocket and withdraws a soft-pack of cigarettes. Lukas watches as her unsteady fingers slide one from the pack. Grasping it between her lips, she fumbles again through her pockets and frowns, apparently unable to locate a match. Lukas is astounded that someone who labors to breath under normal conditions remains so staunchly devoted to smoking. He snatches a box of wooden matches from a drawer beside the refrigerator and lights her cigarette for her. Here's to self-destruction.

Gladys slowly sucks a meager drag from the cigarette, eyeing Lukas all the while with an odd expression. "I don't expect you to understand at your age, kiddo," she states. Here it comes again, Lukas thinks. Another long-winded and banal soliloquy on the subject of aging with no discernable point.

Not without backup.

Lukas retreats two steps toward the kitchen table and reaches into his duffel bag. Pulling out one of the bottles, he turns, grabs a glass from a shelf above the sink, and goes to join Gladys. Silently he curses himself again for having caved in and agreeing to the Thanksgiving dinner plan. He pulls up a chair and sits at the dusty table, pouring himself a glass and readying himself to endure more of Gladys's sentimental meanderings. He is a captive audience. He once more reproaches himself for having agreed to stay here during Susan's trip, but what choice did he have? He's a captive.

Bringing the glass to his lips, he takes dismal notice that his hands quiver worse than do his elderly mother's. Draining almost half the glass's contents with one ambitious gulp, he defies her disapproving expression. He stares pointedly at her cigarette, and she looks away. Fifteen-love.

"At this stage of the game," the old woman says, "the main thing becomes trying to put finishing touches on everything. Straightening all the crooked picture frames that are hanging in your life, I guess you could call it."

The rest of the Scotch looks lonely in the bottom of the small glass, so Lukas welcomes it into his throat. It feels like years have passed since Susan drove off yesterday.

"You remember that little farm upstate where we used to go, the one that lets you pick out a live turkey?"

"Oh, come on, Gladys…" Lukas begins wearily.

"Come on nothing," she spits back. "I said I wanted a traditional Thanksgiving. Now you said you had to go upstate this weekend anyway. You'll be going right by it."

Lukas sinks more heavily into his chair. He is all at once terrorized by the possibility that Gladys will subsist for several more years, that this whole mess will become a yearly chore. "Forget it," he says. "It's ridiculous. I'm sure they've got plenty of turkeys at the Safeway in town. What's the difference?"

"There is no difference, except in my mind. I'm an old woman, but I'm still a woman. I'm allowed to be sentimental. It would mean a lot to me. Plus…," she pauses at this point to draw another slow drag from her cigarette, perhaps stalling to grope for a less-flimsy reason for her request, then says in a meek voice, "… it's not even out of your way."

Lukas sits, scowling at his empty glass.

"You used to love the holidays. It'll be just like old times."

"How can you say that?" an incredulous Lukas demands. There, it's been said. The elephant in the room has been identified.

Gladys looks away. She leans forward and slides a dusty candleholder across the tablecloth toward her. She says nothing for a moment as she taps ashes from the end of her cigarette into it.

The silence is smothering.

After a long moment, Gladys says calmly, "I don't know what went on between you and Stephen."

Lukas feels his heart accelerate. Trying to appear as if he's not hurrying, he fills his glass again, spilling a couple of drops with the hasty and clumsy effort. He says nothing, and with his silence the same burdensome lie is repeated once more. Life, after all, offers countless opportunities and reasons to tell a lie, but rare are the circumstances where the truth will adequately suffice in its place.

She continues, her head down, voice low, "You two were never that close to take his death as hard as you have."

The furnace kicks on and begins to hum, as if trying to fill the harsh quietude that hangs between the two humans who sit miles away from each other at the dining room table.

Knowing Lukas will not respond, Gladys eventually resumes the one-sided conversation. "Of all the things that have gone wrong in my life, there's only one thing I'd change if I could. Just one."

Lukas braces himself. He swallows more whiskey, and it hurries down his throat, searching for the blazing spot that needs soothing, but it can't seem to locate it.

"I'd like to be able to tell Stephen that I love him just one more time," she says in a trembling voice. "Just once more."

Lukas presses a hand to his sternum to try to slow the wild beating of his heart, the pain of which causes him to lean forward heavily against the table. He is aware that his heart is not supposed to be doing what it's doing, and he shudders at the absurdity of the possibility that he may collapse and die right here in front of his frail mother.

Still not looking at her son, Gladys inhales strongly, gathering control over her emotions. "But he's gone," she says in a much firmer voice, "and that's a fact." She takes another drag from her cigarette, glancing at Lukas's wincing expression. "And we're here, and we can't stop living, just because he had to. So we go on the best we can." She nods, as if replaying the statement in her head for verification.

The pain in Lukas's chest begins to lessen, and he finds himself mildly disappointed at the prospect of his surviving to hear the conclusion of yet another one of Gladys's sermons. Perhaps Stephen *had* been the lucky one.

"So now," Gladys says in a slightly more cheerful tone, "a family Thanksgiving means you and me, kiddo. And Susan."

An involuntary grimace flashes across Lukas's face, and not from the fleeting throbbing in his chest. It does not go unnoticed by Gladys.

"I know," she says with a tired sigh. "You're not her biggest fan, for whatever reason. That's your own business, and none of mine."

I'll drink to that, Lukas thinks. And he does.

"But don't forget that you and me aren't the only ones who have to deal with Stephen being gone. I'll never get a chance fix anything that might need fixing between me and him." She pauses and swallows a couple of times, obviously fighting to maintain the stability of her voice. "But I don't intend to leave any doubt in Susan's mind how I feel about her."

Lukas nods in a slow, gloomy admission. "Atonement," he mutters.

Gladys smashes out what little remains of her cigarette among the ashes in the candleholder. "I wouldn't call it that, necessarily," she says evenly. "But I'll grant that there are worse ways to spend one's time." She purses her lips, folds her hands on the table in front of her. "I don't expect you to understand."

But he does. He understands. More acutely than his mother will ever realize. It's why he's here, after all, the willing captive. *Penance* could be the title to his life's story. If it ever comes to a merciful end.

Chapter Twenty-two

Millions of earthquakes occur each year, but only about five hundred thousand of them are strong enough to be picked up by most seismographic instruments. And on average, only about a hundred thousand tremors are strong enough to even be noticed by human beings.

Lukas is in charge of a dozen sensors spread out in strategic positions throughout the county, which function like remote seismographs to measure the motion of the earth's crust. The information that's sent back to Lukas's office is also forwarded electronically to the state observatory center, where it is compacted, recorded, and forwarded again in a nice tidy package to the National Earthquake Information Center in Colorado, where—Lukas is certain—it is added to a humongous file of data that is summarily ignored by everyone who works there. Unless of course the data reaches certain benchmarks which suggest the possibility of an impending quake of any significance.

Lukas leans back in his chair and rereads—for the third time this morning—the latest column of figures he's compiled. Two of the readings fall within the range that would suggest trouble spots, which makes three readings from two separate sensors in the past week. Ordinarily, this kind of result would catch the eye of someone at the state center, and at the very least someone would place a call and ask Lukas some questions, or request further analysis. However, because Lukas is in charge of an area that is not near any tectonic plate edges or known faults, and because constant oil drilling in the area sometimes rattles the frame shafts of his sensors and throws off the data, the state center has gotten into the habit of ignoring most of the data Lukas sends their way, however ostensibly unusual it may seem.

Most of the time Lukas himself would not give such minor blips a second thought. Most of the time.

Having been haunted by the horrific imagery from his recurring nightmare the past few weeks has sent his normal attitude of apathy on an illogical sabbatical. He can't shake the notion that a serious quake is about to happen. Forget the data, something tells him it's true. His unexplainable ability. The curse. The itch.

Lukas lightly taps his pen on the desk, wracked with indecision. Glancing over at the clock, he realizes he should have left a few minutes ago. He's due to make his bi-monthly appearance later today at the Palmieri Geological Survey Center, the state observation center where his data is regularly transmitted and disregarded. Once every two months he is required to file reports in person and attend a lengthy and mind-numbing meeting where he must deliver a brief update, summarizing to his superiors the very same data that their equipment has already received and recorded. A two-and-a-half-hour drive upstate to deliver printed and oral copies of redundant information. Your tax dollars at work.

The purpose of these meetings is to insure that every employee is briefed on the latest advances and updates in seismology, both locally and internationally. It is also an opportunity for peons like Lukas to pose any concerns or questions to the experts in his field. Things that ordinarily might not have been flagged for their attention. Things like the three moderately abnormal readings that his sensors have registered in the past week.

He supposes it's his duty to bring it up today, although he already knows what will happen. They'll ask him to repeat and summarize a month's worth of data that they could just as easily read for themselves. Then they'll smile politely, remind him of the relative commonality of these types of aberrant readings in drilling areas, and advise him to dismiss them as harmless anomalies. Just keep a close eye on it, they'll say, and keep us posted.

He could push the issue, sure. Insist that a team be sent down with more delicate equipment to at least check it out. Try to convince them the danger is real, and imminent. Lives will be lost. Explain that his visions and supernatural clairvoyance tell him so.

Lukas snorts, imagining the pleasure they would take in hiring his replacement, should he even mention such wild delusions.

It's pointless. He'll just keep his mouth shut.

Lukas rises, stuffs the folders into his briefcase. Exiting his office, he flips the light off and scowls, resenting the long drive ahead of him. Resenting his sobriety and the stringent DUI regulations that warrant it. Resenting the arduous meeting he'll have to endure. Resenting the smug colleagues who won't believe in his visions, even if he were to try and explain them. Most of all, resenting the visions themselves, and the cursed soul who must experience them.

***

Almost two hours later, Lukas pulls off the interstate onto a remote exit, squinting at the directions he'd scribbled for himself on a wrinkled scrap of paper. He shakes his head in disbelief that he's actually going through with this. His plan is to stop off at this turkey farm—or market, or whatever it is—on the way to his meeting, pick out the unlucky bird, and have them kill it, pluck it, and get it ready for him while he's at his meeting. That way he can pick it up on his way back and be done with the whole preposterous errand. He decides if he doesn't come upon the place within the next mile he'll get back on the interstate and Gladys will have to make do with a frozen bird from the grocery store.

But in the next instant he spots it. Smithwick's Organic Farm and Pantry. Pulling into the lot, Lukas is shocked by the amount of cars already parked, including ones with out-of-state license plates. Lukas can't fathom why so many people would come so far off the beaten path for the chance to pick out their own animal sacrifice. Human beings are a confounding species.

Minutes later Lukas is standing at a wire fence behind the store, staring into a pen where dozens of plump turkeys pace nervously about. As other people standing at the fence point out a particular bird, one of several workers in tall rubber boots expertly scoops it up and carries it squawking into a nearby barn. Lukas is dismayed by the whole display. They are just birds, after all, yet it seems so depressing.

A single turkey waddling along the fence approaches the spot where Lukas stands. He squats down and looks glumly through the fence at the little bird. Its head darts back and forth, obviously alarmed by all the activity. Perhaps it's just now realizing that its entire existence serves only to benefit others. Lukas sees—or imagines he sees—a look of betrayal on the turkey's face, as if it were trying to convey that this fate was not what it had signed on for.

A lump forms in Lukas's throat. "I can relate, little friend," he laments.

Lukas had never come along on this trek with his mother when he was young; he had not prepared himself for the possibility that this place would be so oppressively sad. He wishes for a moment that there was something he could do, but he feels foolish and reminds himself that these are just animals. He wishes he'd had the nerve to refuse to come here for Gladys. He resents her for asking it of him. He wants to leave. He longs for a drink.

He looks back into the doleful eyes of the little turkey. Of course, there is something he can do to help. At least one of them.

"Don't worry," he whispers. "It'll all be over soon."

He stands and nods to a nearby employee, who comes over and gives him a ticket stub, then snatches the turkey as it tries to scurry away and carries it toward the barn. Lukas doesn't stay to watch. He heads around the corner of the building, making space between himself and the turkey pen as fast as possible.

Inside, Lukas opts to pay the extra money to have the bird delivered, rather than having to return to this wretched place. He fills out the delivery forms, and the man at the counter hands him a receipt to take over to the register, where the cashier will ring him up. Then it will all be over.

Waiting in line at the cash register, Lukas thinks ironically that his meeting might not seem so bad after this. Somehow, the thought does not comfort him. He feels himself perspire in his anxiety to leave this place. Something is very wrong.

The itch.

It's even worse in here than it was outside. Lukas unbuttons the top button of his shirt and mops sweat from his forehead with his sleeve.

The woman in front of him has an unreasonable amount of groceries, and it's taking the cashier a painfully long time to ring them up.

The cashier!

That's who's causing it. Lukas looks away, tries to fight off the itch. It's no use. The cashier, probably a couple of years younger than himself, rings up each item with a set jaw, meticulously applied makeup and a blank expression on her face. Lukas can see her pain as clearly as if it were printed on a sign hanging around her neck. She hates being here, feels the job is beneath her dignity, wishes she could be anywhere else at this moment. So does Lukas. The woman in front of him produces a checkbook from her purse. Lukas winces. He has an impulse to drop the receipt and walk out of the store. He closes his eyes and rubs them furiously, trying to ward off the images forming in his head. The lights of a busy city street. The itch has caught him off-guard. Without alcohol as his guardian, he's at the mercy of his visions. It's not fair.

He tries to console himself with the knowledge that the little turkey he picked out of the pen has probably been relieved of its suffering by now. At least he was able to save one damned creature today.

The woman finally completes her purchase and pushes her cart off toward the exit. Lukas gratefully passes the cashier his receipt for the turkey with a trembling hand. He doesn't look at her. He tries to block out what he can see about her. Her longing for a fresh start to a game she's losing.

Handing her a small wad of bills, he tells her to keep the change. Glancing at the name printed on her plastic nametag, he thinks, Sorry, Nora, but I can't save everybody, and he scurries out of the store.

Later that afternoon, Lukas doesn't speak a word to his colleagues about the earthquake he suspects will soon ravage his hometown. You can't save everybody.

Chapter Twenty-three

It's approaching four o'clock when Lukas hears the first stirrings of far off thunder. He nods his head, as if he'd been expecting it. Nothing good happens in the rain.

Lukas lifts his glass and toasts the weather. He declares aloud, for no particular reason, in a voice that's musical and drowsy, "What I'm thankful for is that today only comes once a year."

He looks once more across the dim parlor to the front door, stares hard at it. He decides he'll be ready to leave after one more drink. Maybe not ready, but at least able.

Leaning forward to refill his glass, he hears the front door rattle and looks over skeptically. He imagines momentarily that the door is opening itself to hurry Lukas through it, having grown impatient with his procrastination. But it swings open wide, and Katie steps into the alcove, closing the door and stepping lightly out of her shoes. She keeps the toes of her bare feet splayed slightly above the cold stone surface of the floor. A few early raindrops have darkened a scattering of spots on her green university sweatshirt. Brushing her hair out of her face, she spots Lukas on the sofa and smiles at him.

He raises a glass in her direction. "Happy Thanksgiving," he announces.

Her grin widens, and the lonesome dimple makes its appearance. "Same to you," she says, amused. She pauses in the parlor doorway and readjusts the knapsack hanging from her shoulder. "Celebrating early?"

His voice lowers in volume. "Just getting ready for dinner." He looks at the drink in his hand and takes a sip, looks back at her. "Want to join me?" he says, and catches his breath, abruptly aware of how much he wants her to say yes.

Maintaining her smile, she says, in a way that manages not to sound condescending or judgmental, "It's a little early for me. Going to your mother's for dinner?"

Lukas nods, leans back into the sofa cushion. "How about you?"

Katie twitches her lip, and her smile lessens. "Not this year." She shrugs, and as usual Lukas has no idea how to interpret the gesture. He can feel the slight tingling sensation he feels whenever Katie is around—the itch trying to get his attention—but he doesn't mind. The alcohol has his head blissfully swirling, and besides, he has come to realize that he genuinely enjoys being around Katie, despite the abstract discomfort she may cause him.

A thought occurs to Lukas. A hopeful anticipation bursts into his mind like a prisoner discovering a loose brick in his cell's wall. "You..."

he begins clumsily, "Would you want to come with me? For dinner?" He looks straight at her, his eyes pleading. If she came along, he reasons, he might—better than *might*, most probably *would*—be able to survive the ordeal. A prolonged silence on her part causes him to add, "At my mom's?" Dumb, he thinks.

Katie hesitates a moment longer. She inclines her head a few degrees to one side. "I'm sorry. I would, I really would, but it's … I've got … something I have to do." Her answer sounds as if she had perfectly understood that his question had been the request of a personal favor, not merely a hospitable invite. Sagacious Katie.

Lukas nods and returns his gloomy gaze to the drink in his hand. *Just you and me, pal.*

"What time are you supposed to be there?"

"About twenty minutes ago." He glances at her, sees her raise her eyebrows expectantly, much to his chagrin. He feels timid. "These sort of family things, they're not really my cup of tea."

Katie smiles again, and Lukas can hear it from where he sits. "Hence the cup of whiskey," she says.

Lukas feels a slight grin spread his lips. "Hence the several cups."

Katie snorts. "Sounds like holidays at my house."

Lukas looks back at the door. He stays put. "How'd you get out of it?" he says, more to prolong the conversation than out of authentic curiosity.

Katie heaves a quick breath, lets it out audibly. "I had a good excuse this year; I actually have something important to do." She hesitates, starting to form a word with her lips, but then changing direction. "But as it turns out, I didn't end up having to use it. My mother didn't ask. She's off on a trip with some guy." She shrugs and rolls her eyes. "She thinks that if she finds the right man, everything else in her life will fall into place. But anyway, it gets me off the hook."

Lukas is confused by the mixture of disappointment and relief in her voice. He doesn't know how to respond, so he says nothing. Lukas is dismayed by his apparent conversational handicap; trying to talk with others invariably makes him feel ill-equipped, like someone who only reads the Sunday comics trying to hold a literary discussion with a Chaucer expert.

"Are you gonna go," Katie asks.

Lukas blushes, realizing that he *had* actually been considering skipping it altogether. He is continually unnerved by Katie's uncanny sense of perception. He shrugs. "I guess I kind of have to."

"You don't have to," Katie says, "but you should."

He looks over at her briefly, then back to his drink. He takes another sip.

"As much as it sucks to be around your family sometimes," Katie says mildly, "it's cool to know that they want you there. They're still your family."

Lukas suspects that she's not talking about him and his mother. Could this be part of the explanation for the itch, then? A vague idea forms in his mind about Katie's recent birthday.

"Being there for someone when they need you—without them having to say that they need you—that's the best gift you can give a person," Katie says, gently fingering the bracelet on her wrist. "As you know," she adds softly.

Lukas casts a quick look at her and immediately averts his gaze. He doesn't know what she's referring to, and her compassionate expression makes him uneasy. He drains the remaining whiskey from his glass, avoiding the stare of Confusing Katie.

"I'll tell you what," she says, her tone lightening, "you go have dinner with your mom, and I'll meet you back here at ten. Bottle of wine, my treat. You can tell me all the horror stories."

Lukas casts a quick look at the clock. That's six hours from now. One bottle of wine might not be enough. He feels his face soften. "You're on," he hears himself say, without looking over at her.

Katie turns and begins climbing the stairs to her room. Before she disappears from view she calls out, "Good luck!" Lukas is surprised to realize he's smiling, feeling as though he already has it.

***

They had both tried to persuade Lukas to carve the turkey, but he had firmly refused, citing his badly shaking hands. But really, it had been his memory of the creature's melancholy eyes when it had been alive. And also the whole idea of the ritual. The father—the head of the household— in the Norman Rockwell painting. The center of attention. Although, truth be told, Lukas still feels he is the center of attention at the table. He has somehow become the outsider. He notices the knowing glances that pass between his mother and Susan, the easy way with which they talk and laugh with each other. Susan has deftly managed to become more a part of his own family than he is.

Lukas refills his glass with Chardonnay. He doesn't try to hide or downplay how much he's drinking, despite the disapproving glares that keep coming his way. There's no point in trying to hide, after all, when you're one-third of a room's total population.

The wind outside has gathered strength, and it carries the rain sideways so that it smacks against the dining room window. Serious rain. Purposeful.

"My goodness," Gladys remarks.

"I suppose we need it," says Susan. "The whole country seems to be getting it." She clears her throat and smiles, turning slightly toward Lukas. "Luke, did you see those poor balloon handlers at the parade this morning?"

Lukas pushes a cut piece of turkey across his plate with a fork. "Uh, no," he says without looking up.

"He doesn't have a TV set," Gladys explains.

The turkey died in vain. He has come out dry, tough. A wasted life.

"Well," Susan says, "the wind started to pick up toward the end of the parade in New York. It looked like it might carry off a couple of those giant balloons, and take the poor little guys holding the strings off with it!"

Gladys and Susan both chuckle quietly towards each other at the memory of the image. Their own private joke. Lukas takes a bite of mashed potatoes and pretends to chew thoughtfully. This is how it's going to be, then, every year. A precedent has been set. Lukas rues his foolish decision to agree to this dinner, for now it will become a yearly expectation. Gladys will continue to defy medical science and survive to insist on this same meal for years to come. And Lukas will continue to acquiesce in his typical cowardly fashion. At least he'd had the guts right before dinner to refuse when his mother had suggested they attend a campus event together. One of the dance recitals or concert performances, she'd said. But he had held firm, put his foot down. And it hadn't been that difficult. So why couldn't he have summoned that kind of resolve when she'd insisted on this dinner idea? He tips his glass and furiously chugs the rest of his wine like a marathon runner with a glass of ice water.

He reaches for the bottle to pour himself another.

"Good idea," Gladys says. "Let's have a toast."

Lukas pours an unsteady glassful and waits.

"Well, this might turn out to be my last Thanksgiving," Gladys says.

"Oh Mom, stop," Susan chides, looking down at her own glass.

Lukas glances over at Susan, raising one eyebrow. *Mom?*

"Oh hush up," Gladys says. "Facts are facts. I just want to raise a toast to family. Those of us here, I'm glad we could all be together." She looks tenderly at Susan, then at Lukas, who is unable to return the look. Then she lifts her gaze toward the ceiling. "And for those that have left us," she continues more softly. Lukas and Susan both look down at the half-finished meals on their plates. "May God take good care of them, until we can all be together once more." She hesitates, as if she wants to say more, but instead she clamps her lips together, nods, and takes a sip of wine. After a moment's delay, Susan does the same. Lukas doesn't.

Maybe there is a heaven. Maybe Stephen is up there right now, watching them. Lukas does not relish the possibility of having to face his brother again. Heaven could turn out to be pure hell. Still, Lukas reasons, it can't be much worse than this.

It's a chance he's willing to take because there's also the possibility that nothing at all happens. When you die, everything stops. Like going to sleep. No more itch, no more responsibility, no more regret. Just sleep. Resting in peace. Lukas longs for it so badly that he feels real physical pain. A fire bubbling in his belly. One he won't extinguish until after his mother has passed on. A hard promise, but he holds firm. He knows he's a warped and heartless person, but even he won't subject his mother to having to witness the deaths of both of her offspring. No one should have to go through that, not even Gladys. So he waits.

And he drinks.

***

The rest of the torturous meal had evaporated in a wine-flavored haze. After Gladys's toast, the conversation between her and Susan had become more subdued. And Lukas had continued to sit there sedately, drinking steadily and rearranging the food on his plate, trying to answer their occasional questions politely and coherently. And finally the meal and its trappings had humanely come to an end.

Lukas had of course helped clean up afterward. He had managed to only drop one plate between the dining room and kitchen, and he had cleaned up the pieces swiftly and expertly.

Later Susan had helped Gladys up the stairs to get ready for bed. Lukas had sat back down at the dining room table to wait for ten o'clock to arrive. He had become aware that he was much more drunk than he had thought. Too drunk even to drive across town back to his house, which for Lukas was very, very drunk indeed.

Sitting slumped at the dining room table with his back to the kitchen, Lukas wishes to be back on his sofa. He wants to see Katie. He decides that a tall glass of water might help him regain his bearings, but his legs have become extremely heavy. The kitchen feels far away.

A glass of water appears out of nowhere on the table in front of him. At first, Lukas is not sure it's real, but then he sees Susan standing beside him.

Cornered.

Lukas reaches unsteadily for the water, feeling his pulse accelerate. There are very few people that Lukas feels at ease being alone with. In fact, the list consists of only one. And her name isn't Susan.

Lukas swallows too much water and sputters a cough. Susan makes her way tentatively around the table and silently takes a seat at the head of the table, perpendicular to where he sits. Not the traditional interrogation setup, but Lukas begins to sweat nonetheless. Both of them fix their gazes on spots off to the side rather than at each other. For an arrested moment, neither speaks.

Susan utters a short, nervous laugh. "I think I may have overcooked the turkey a little bit," she says.

Lukas sneaks a quick glance at the clock. Still not close enough to ten o'clock. "Is Gladys off to bed?"

"Mm-hmm."

Lukas turns the glass of ice-water in a slow rotation on the table in front of him. Susan folds her arms across her chest, then unfolds them and places them on her lap. After a moment she clears her throat. "It's been a long time since you and I have been alone together." Lukas shoots an alarmed look at her, and immediately she reddens. "I-I mean … I didn't mean it … like *that*." She shifts in her chair. "It was nice of you to come over, Luke."

Lukas begins to bring his glass to his lips, but he's embarrassed by the shaking, so he sets it back down. "Gladys is getting sentimental in her old age," he says.

Susan nods. "I know it wasn't easy for you," she continues, without looking at him. "It's not easy for me, either."

Lukas looks again at the clock, which appears not to be advancing at all. He indicates the empty wine bottle on a nearby counter. "Alcohol helps," he says, in a doomed attempt to sound light-hearted.

Susan looks down at her lap and smiles without humor. "I know it seems to."

Lukas senses an impending rebuke and steels himself for it.

"I've been clean now for … it'll be four years next month," Susan says, her voice soft and growing softer. "I know how you feel, probably better than anyone else."

Lukas stares hard at the condensation on his glass. Attempts at empathy prickle him. His lips purse and his free hand balls into a fist. "You don't know the half of it."

"When he," Susan begins, but her voice cracks and she stops. She keeps her eyes glued on her lap through a long silence. When she finally speaks again, her voice is subdued, but unwavering. "For a long time afterwards, I felt lost. Just completely lost." She nods to herself, choosing her words carefully. "It was as if everything … unraveled—so quickly—and I had no backup plan."

She looks over at Lukas, and he can feel her look, but he won't return it. He won't risk another look at the clock either, afraid of finding the hands moving backwards.

Folding her arms on the table in front of her, Susan leans toward Lukas. "We made a *terrible* mistake. But there's nothing we can do about it now. We just need to move on." She swallows a couple of times. She looks hard at Lukas, and her chin is trembling. "That's what I'm trying to do, anyway ... finally," she says, her voice now no more than a whisper. "That's why I'm trying to become an RN, trying to get my head straight. It's time to move on."

Lukas feels his eyes filling with tears that have been missing for almost two decades. "I don't know how," he whispers.

A tear drips from each of Susan's eyes, and she whisks them away with her quivering hands. She nods, trying to summon her voice. "I know," is all she can muster.

Lukas is hypnotized by the tingling coolness of the lone teardrop that snakes its way down his cheek. It's an odd sensation, at once foreign and familiar, remembered from a lifetime ago.

"We're all three trying to find our way, Luke. There's no sense in trying to do it all alone." She dares to reach across the table.

Lukas looks through blurred eyes at her delicate outstretched hand, ardent and pleading. But he won't take it. Because there are some places you can only go alone.

He pushes himself back from the table and stands.

Looking at the floor, he shifts his weight to one foot, then the other, searching his vocabulary for words that just aren't there. "I'm sorry," are the only whispered sentiments that manage to emerge. Then he turns and hurries toward the front door.

Away from her.

Chapter Twenty-four

Three days.

It has been three whole days since Lukas was last asleep. Watching the clock on his desk approach the top of the hour, he figures the math in his head. Seventy-two hours have elapsed since the last day Lukas had been able to sleep. Extremely unusual, even for him. Not the insomnia, that's par for the course, but usually he can render himself unconscious simply by consuming enough alcohol. During the past three days that hasn't worked. Lukas has swallowed an amount of whiskey that could kill a smaller man, yet he remains awake. Playing tag with sleep, and he's "It."

He lifts his hand and covers his left eye, trying to bring the clock into clearer focus. He winces at the sting he feels as his eyelid closes. Since the previous afternoon, Lukas has kept a bottle of Visine in his shirt pocket, reaching for it frequently in a vain attempt to soothe his burning, sleep-deprived eyes. Every couple of hours he reapplies the drops—which is a comically messy procedure, thanks to his shaky hands—to little effect. His dry, bleary eyes greedily soak in the liquid supplement and then immediately revert back to their parched state.

Lukas sits up straighter in his chair and tries to collect his meandering thoughts and steer them in a cohesive direction. When your body is denied sleep for too long, you find yourself wandering mechanically through the routines of your life. You spend minutes at a time staring at mundane objects like a pencil jar or the side of a cabinet, not comprehending what you're looking at, but not aware enough to stop yourself from staring.

This morning Lukas had decided to make an appearance at his office for the first time since before the holiday, figuring if he's not able to sleep anyway he might as well attempt to accomplish something useful while he's awake. The wrenching conversation with Susan on Thursday night remains engraved in his mind, but everything since that point hovers without definition around his consciousness, like disconnected scenes from a movie edited in haphazard manner with no discernable plot. He had not made it back that night for his arranged ten o'clock meeting with Katie, but he is at a loss to explain why not. There had been an uncertain amount of hours spent sitting in his car at the park, sipping from a bottle of Jameson and watching the thunderstorm ravage the area. He is unsure how long the rain and tempests that began on Thanksgiving had lasted, but after rising from his sleepless bed the next morning, the sight of its lingering fury through the kitchen window had been enough to deter him from showing up at work. He works alone, and still he wouldn't win Employee of the Month.

The office appears unchanged, seeming not to have noticed his absence, and Lukas finds himself entertaining abstract thoughts about his relative insignificance in the world, how people would still carry umbrellas if there were one fewer raindrop, when he gradually becomes aware of an unusual beeping sound, emanating intermittently from somewhere behind him. Lukas swivels groggily in his chair to try to locate the source of the noise. The monitor of the computer on the other desk is dark, but the green power button glowing on the console indicates that the computer itself is still on, hibernating in sleep mode. Lukas sits motionless, listening. After a moment, another beep confirms that it is coming from the computer he suspected, so he rolls his chair over to face it and presses the keyboard's space bar to reactivate the display. The monitor immediately comes back to life and reveals an error message clamoring for his attention.

Squinting, Lukas reads the message's code and scans over the other information. It appears that sometime during his absence, the building had temporarily lost power. Lukas has all his equipment set to automatically resume its functioning once power is restored, but this message is apparently telling him the electrical interruption has somehow caused a transmission error that the system is unable to fix on its own.

In his muddled mental state, Lukas is unable to determine exactly what the message is attempting to convey to him. He rereads it twice more, but has no idea what it means. It looks like a jumble of technical jargon, random words arranged to look like a sentence, but without meaning.

Lukas sighs. He is from a generation that seems uniformly disenchanted with technology, but he could be their leader. To him it feels like the equipment in this office is more trouble than it's worth, that he spends more time attempting to fix it than he does gaining any valuable information from it. Nothing but flat tires along the information superhighway. Disgusted, he pushes himself out of his chair to go see what other equipment has decided to fail while he was away.

Standing causes a sudden head rush. He loses his balance and immediately sits back down. A wave of nausea passes over him, and he takes a deep breath to try to extinguish it. Because of his diet—or at least the inordinate percentage of it that's liquid—Lukas's stomach is in a constant state of mild agitation, but over the past three days he has felt increasingly queasy with each hour that passes without sleep. A constant pressure has settled into his temples and forehead. It's not what people call a "pounding" headache. Rather, his head feels stretched, as if unseen forces were holding him by his hair a few inches off the ground.

Trying again, he is able to successfully stand, and he moves over to inspect the mounds of printouts that have collected on the floor beside the seismographs. His eyes scan across the jagged lines of blue ink, but his mind wanders. He is a pathetic, pitiful creature. Where is the wisdom in someone who consumes alcohol to make himself feel better mentally, when it only results in making him feel much worse physically? Lukas is continually astonished by his colossal stupidity.

He stops.

This can't be right. Lukas backtracks over the data he's just read and double-checks the corresponding figures at the bottom of each column. He tears a sheet from the printout and takes it back to his desk. He rubs his eyes and then stretches them open wide, trying to clear his blurry vision. He flips on the desk lamp and studies the printout once more. This has to be another faulty reading, he decides.

The data he's looking at suggests that a tremor of unusual magnitude occurred sometime during the time Lukas was out of the office.

"This can't be right," he says aloud. "I would have felt it."

Most earthquakes that occur aren't even strong enough to be picked up by his outdated equipment, but if the information Lukas is looking at is correct, it should have not only been picked up by the sensors, but people walking around would have been able to feel it. He looks back at the numbers in the top left corner of the column. It takes his frazzled mind longer than usual to convert them, but he soon deduces that the printout he's holding registered just before noon on Friday. Two days ago. Impossible. Lukas struggles to think back to Friday, to distinguish it from the hazy menagerie that the past few days have combined themselves into within his memory. After a moment, it comes to him. Friday morning was when he decided not to come in because of the intensity of the thunderstorm. The whole house had seemed to shudder beneath the thunder and ferocious winds. Lukas feels his heartbeat accelerate. It is possible, then, that a tremor like this might have occurred, but he hadn't noticed it amid all the chaos of the storm. Which means the printout in front of him is more than likely correct.

Lukas hadn't realized it until this moment, but one blessing of his insomnia had been that his lack of sleep had prevented him from having had to endure his recurring nightmare about the earthquake at the university. But now, looking at the sobering printout on his desk, the horrific details from the dream flash across his mind and send a cold shiver scampering up his back.

The readings from his sensors are frequently wrong, and he is used to being ignored and condescended to by the arrogant scientists at the State

Observatory Center, but Lukas finds it incomprehensible that they would dismiss a reading like this. Even if it's wrong, the numbers themselves would have to warrant a closer examination, or further tests, and he hadn't received so much as a phone call? It doesn't make any sense.

Lukas has long speculated that a fault lies hidden somewhere deep beneath this town, one that's not on any of the maps or charts. Or possibly a hot spot in the upper mantle, like the one that lies beneath Yellowstone Park. Maybe too much rock is melting into magma, and the ground itself will soon settle into a new position. He has always felt that oil drilling alone would not cause the wildly inconsistent readings that his sensors frequently register. Of course his superiors had never shown any interest in his theories, so he has for the most part kept them to himself. After all, there's not really a way to explain why he thinks he's right, any more than there's a rational way to explain how he knows any of the other things he knows. Things that normal people couldn't, and shouldn't, know. But if Lukas is correct, and a tectonic event is about to happen, then Friday's readout could have been an authentic foreshock, which means the things he's witnessed in that nightmare may be more than just a bad dream.

Lukas shakes his head stiffly. He's just being paranoid. These are frightful delusions, that's all. Too much alcohol and not enough sleep. Still, it's extremely odd that no one from the State Observatory Center had bothered to call him and ask about the unusual numbers. That kind of negligence goes against every standard operating procedure that exists.

Unless, of course, they hadn't received the data.

Lukas rolls over to the monitor that displays the error message and reads it again. Suddenly its meaning becomes clear to him. It's telling him that once power was restored, the transmitter failed to come back online. Which means none of this data has been sent to the SOC. Lukas swallows hard, feeling another wave of nausea rise up within him. This had happened once before, a couple of years ago. The transmitter had stopped working, and until it got repaired, Lukas had had to transmit all the data manually.

And that is precisely what he should have been doing for the past three days. None of these readouts had been transmitted because he had not been here to send them. Lukas leans on his desk and rests his head in his hands. He'll catch holy hell for this. His weary mind tries to conjure up excuses to get him off the hook. He'll say the thunderstorm fried his fax machine. But then they will just point out that he should have emailed the data. Why hadn't anyone called to find out why no data was being sent? Were they waiting for him to stumble so they could finally replace him? It appears as if now they will have their chance.

No matter what will happen to him, the fact remains that they must be made aware of Friday's data. If it turns out to be as dire a situation as Lukas suspects, he will undoubtedly be fired. Perhaps he will even face some sort of criminal charges of negligence, but at the very least he'll be jobless. There's no avoiding that now. Lukas stares for a long time at the phone before he reaches for it. He tries to think of what he will say, but nothing comes to mind. He is surprised to realize he's not really filled with the dread that he expected. He feels numb, more than anything else. Exhausted. Spent and indifferent.

He reaches for the phone, but his hand stops. Lukas looks at his hand with wonder. He hadn't consciously willed it to stop before reaching the phone; it's as if the appendage is functioning on its own. Then, Lukas catches his breath, aware of something else. It's rising inside him, slicing its way through his blinding headache, over the boiling nausea. The itch. It creeps along an invisible icy path under his skin.

Lukas can't make any sense of it. It's more unspecific than usual, just a general sense of disturbance. He pulls his hand back and glares at the phone. The State needs to be alerted right away. The reading could be nothing, just another aberrant and faulty result, but it could indicate that a major quake is likely to hit, something deadly like what he's seen in his recurring dream. The SOC would send some specialists down right away to investigate. If need be, they would be able to warn people, possibly save lives.

So why hasn't Lukas called? Is it because he's afraid of losing his job, or is it something worse?

Lukas scowls, frustrated by what he assumes is his continuing gradual descent into madness. Just get it over with already. He decides to walk across the street and get a cup of coffee. The fresh air and caffeine might help clear his head. Then he'll be able to figure out what he should say when he calls.

He rises unsteadily and heads out his office door. Immediately upon being confronted with the crisp chill of the morning air, he remembers his jacket that he left hanging on the back of his chair. Fall has been served its eviction notice, and winter's ready to move in. He doesn't bother going back for the coat, just quickens his pace and scurries across the street to the coffee stand. There is another customer in line, an old man counting out change on the counter in a slow and deliberate fashion, as if it's a foreign currency he's never seen. Lukas scans the meager display of prepackaged muffins and sweets. The very thought makes him squeamish, so he just grabs the largest styrofoam cup available and begins filling it from a steaming pot. It's not the kind you pour, it's the kind you hold your cup underneath and press a button to dispense the coffee. This takes longer than Lukas had hoped for, and he allows his gaze to drift across the headlines of the Sunday newspapers.

Suddenly Lukas is unable to breathe. There, near the bottom right corner of the front page of the local edition, is a full color photograph of an enormous Christmas tree. Lukas's hands erupt into convulsions. *It's the tree he has seen countless times in his nightmare.*

Lukas sets his almost-full cup of coffee on the counter. His still trembling hands pick up the paper. The article states that one of the oldest pine trees on the university's campus was felled by a lightning bolt during the recent thunderstorms, but most of it was able to be salvaged, and it was then squeezed inside the iconic Longkesh Music Hall. Student volunteers have decorated it, and it now adorns the stage.

Despite the cold, late November air, Lukas can feel drops of sweat running down his forehead. With an other-worldly dread slowly beginning to smother him, Lukas continues reading and finds out that the ceremonial lighting of the immense tree is scheduled to take place prior to the University's annual winter concert on this coming Friday evening.

With the haunted stare of a man who has just witnessed his own funeral, Lukas backs away from the coffee stand, allowing the newspaper to drop back onto its pile. The vendor, a lanky, pale fellow bundled in several layers of clothing, regards Lukas with a quizzical look.

Lukas takes a few more steps backwards, unable to pry his gaze from the newspaper. The vendor calls out, "What about your coffee?" But his words don't matter to Lukas, who has now turned and begun retreating back across the street. A pick-up truck and an S.U.V. both must brake hard to avoid him, and the drivers serenade Lukas with an angry chorus of blaring horns, which he ignores in his numbed stupor.

As Lukas steps back inside his office, he stops. He is startled to realize the expression on his face somewhat resembles a smile. With the suddenness of driving beneath an overpass during a rainstorm, clarity has emerged for Lukas. He shakes his head, almost amused at how simply it appears he will be able to fix things—everything—all at once. Now he knows exactly what to say when he calls.

With renewed vigor, Lukas scampers into position at his desk, in a rush to start repairing his broken life, trying to decide what to fix first. He reaches for the data printout.

Part Three

Chapter Twenty-five

It's late. Most of the windows in the buildings on campus are dark, reflecting the vacant hush that only occurs on holiday breaks. Katie slouches at a silent piano in the basement practice studio of the music hall, profoundly alone. She sweeps her left hand absently along the polished keys, not applying enough pressure to make them strike their notes, but enough to feel their cool, smooth texture against her fingertips. Disorganized sheet music is propped and paper-clipped before her, but she has yet to play a single note. Her thoughts have wandered far from music.

She is thinking about Brendan. More specifically, she is trying to probe herself for the real reason she hasn't attempted to contact him for almost a week. He is undeniably attractive, a rare mixture of delicate features and disheveled ruggedness. Sure, he's bigger and stronger than she is, but hadn't she already vowed that she wouldn't let negative experiences from her past affect her present? She has no reason not to trust him; he's not the aggressive type. He makes her laugh. His upbeat outlook contrasts nicely with her personality, which all too often descends into cynical pessimism. He would be good for her. She reminds herself of this fact regularly, adding that the probability of her finding someone better is unlikely at best. Her friends enthusiastically approve of him. On paper, as the expression goes, he's perfect for her.

Trouble is, she reasons, life is not lived on paper. It has nothing to do with her trust issues; she is simply unable to summon a genuine desire for him. Yet she can't rationalize why, and this angers her. Normal people long for a meaningful relationship with a guy like Brendan, so why can't she? Her mother is probably right. With effort, she might be able to make things work with him, and maybe that really *is* the nature of relationships.

Everyone has things about themselves they don't like, that they wish they could change. Near the top of Katie's list is her introspective nature. She yearns to understand her own motives and desires, to be able to explain why she does the things she does. She is frustrated by her perpetual failure to do so. Her perplexing indifference to Brendan is simply the latest in a long line of mysteries about her own psyche that she's been unable to solve. She suspects that her failure to understand herself—in the indubitable, Socratic way—has been the single most prominent contributor to her near-constant state of being wracked with indecision—another aspect of her nature she finds difficult to tolerate. She feels as if she's stuck sitting at a green light, getting nowhere because she can't decide whether to turn right or left.

Part of her senses that a relationship with Brendan could turn out to be inconceivably rewarding, but a louder voice tells her that he's not right for her at all. She continues to hesitate, instead of merely accepting the prudence of the louder voice—partly out of a fear of hurting his feelings. She does feel some sort of affection for him, and it would sadden her to cause him to feel rejected.

She's no stranger to feeling rejected, after all. She suspects her mother is largely to blame for this. This is one facet of her personality that Katie does feel she has a pretty solid handle on. Her mother's steadfast refusal to believe what had happened with Craig had been devastating. Not only had Nora been unwilling to accept even the slightest responsibility for what had occurred, she had withheld the validation and consolation that a mother owes her daughter by disputing the truth of Katie's allegations. To a young girl, it had been the ultimate rejection. She had been made to feel that any attempt to bring it up in conversation would be seen as an insult to her mother. Even now it remains the most conspicuous of the many elephants in the room of their relationship.

Gradually, over the past three years, she has also come to understand that she's turned out to be a disappointment to her mother, that she'd always been so, as a matter of fact. She's not sure why or how it happened, but she's become convinced of it. Having a vague sense of having already fallen short of expectations is what has birthed in her such intensive dread of failure. She's consumed with trying to shield herself from its blight by developing a laid-back and detached, even-keel personality.

As a child she hadn't understood this or been able to define it, but one of the great tragedies of being a child is the ability to be scarred by something even though you can't fathom it. In retrospect Katie has been able to identify a number of decisions she'd made that had been motivated by an unconscious desire to gain her mother's approval. Once she had reached this epiphany she had guarded closely against it, determined not to let it become an influential factor in any future decisions.

She often wonders if the promise she's made to herself is one that's beyond her power to control, one that will continue to be impossible to keep. All it has resulted in so far has been an increased reactionary resentment against her mother, which has put further strain on their already contentious relationship. But deep down Katie will always long for her mother's acceptance, no matter how little esteem she holds for her.

Katie sighs, reaches and taps a C-note, scarcely aware that she's doing it. If only she could be certain about Brendan. Then she could end it right away, for false hope is toxic, and it acts without preference or conscience, and it certainly doesn't need her for an accomplice if it decides to train its sights on Brendan. Then again, perhaps she should stick it out with him for a bit; give it a chance to grow into something real. She's frightened of making the wrong decision, which has once again locked her up in her typical position of not being able to decide anything at all.

Even if she was sure of it, she reminds herself grimly, breaking up with him will still cause him pain. The decision then would become whether to hurt him sooner or later. Not much of a choice. Another cruel reminder of life's tendency to lure you into situations where all the options that might produce a positive outcome are suddenly taken off the table, and all you're left with is choosing whom you will injure, and how much. Choose your weapon carefully.

Katie wags her head in slow, glum frustration. It seems there can be no avoiding making poor Brendan feel like …

A thought stuns her. She snatches her fingers away from the keys as if stung by a hornet. *To make him feel like Lukas has made* me *feel.*

Katie hadn't allowed herself to contemplate how much Lukas had hurt her feelings by not showing up that night. Thanksgiving night. How she had sat in the parlor, reading a magazine, waiting for him to arrive, the sickening, familiar feeling of being forgotten steadily growing inside her with each passing minute. She had ended up finishing the bottle of Cabernet by herself, had fallen asleep before she could identify the particulars of what exactly she was feeling. And then in the morning she'd been too distracted by a piercing headache and the rampaging thunderstorm to do so. But now it's clear. No matter how much she's tried to reach out to him, to be a friend to him, he keeps making it clear that she's not even a blip on his radar. So why does she keep trying? There's something about him. Katie, who hasn't felt comfortable alone with any man since she was eight years old, genuinely likes to be around Lukas. She's not sure why, but he makes her feel safe. In a way that Brendan doesn't. Even more importantly, though, Lukas makes her feel less different, less alone, in a way nobody else ever has.

Or, she wonders, does she try to befriend him merely out of pity? Without a doubt he's a lonely, broken man, easy to feel sympathy for. But it occurs to her that perhaps he's brought this on himself. Could be he's always been as cold to others as he's been to her, and loneliness is precisely what he deserves.

She decides to stop thinking about him, to willfully force him out of her mind whenever thoughts about him sneak in. He's not worth it, after all. Katie admonishes herself for wanting affection from him, friendship even.

Time to grow up, Reiker, she warns herself. Why do you keep waiting for someone to come along and save you? It's not Lukas's job, any more than it's Nora's job, or Brendan's. It's time to save yourself. Past time, dammit.

While she had been scolding herself, Katie's fingers had found their way to the piano's keys, absently striking notes. First one, then another, a C here, an F flat there. Then, in the dim light of the studio, the reverberating notes begin to recognize one another, like old acquaintances at a cocktail party, and they start to align themselves together. Soon Katie is playing a song. Not one she's ever seen, not one that even exists on sheet music, but one she's known all her life. And in that formerly quiet, forsaken studio, Katie—who had moments ago firmly decided to stop looking for answers—begins to take the first steps toward finding them.

Chapter Twenty-Six

That night, some eighty-five hours since Lukas Willow had last been asleep, he stands leaning against the bathroom countertop, examining his reflection in the only mirror in the house. It's the first time he's taken a close look at himself in at least a decade. The years have been cruel to you, he thinks. He rotates his head slowly to one side, then the other. Deserved retribution, he supposes.

He's well on his way to becoming a bald man. He observes this without disappointment, without any particular emotional reaction, really. No wistful nostalgia, just an objective damage assessment. The whiskers he's neglected for the past two days are coming in crudely, and the silver ones far outnumber the brown. There is no longer a well-defined jaw line separating his face from his neck; the two areas have reached lazily toward one another and now connect in a gradual slope.

But what seems most peculiar are his eyes. Lukas seems to remember them having been a different color. A lighter shade of gray, perhaps. Or it could be that his memory just isn't as reliable as it used to be. Like his knees. Either way, it's alarmingly disconcerting to look into a mirror and not recognize yourself. Lukas imagines that once the house belongs to Katie, she'll put up more mirrors. One in every room, maybe. And why not? She has a much more satisfying view to enjoy.

Lukas scrutinizes the unfamiliar gray eyes in the mirror. They grow wider. He shivers with sudden recognition.

They are the impenetrable eyes of a man, he realizes, who is evil.

He swallows hard. He could close his eyes, but the ones in the mirror would still be there. He nods at himself with the solemn conviction of an expert. It's true, then. No one who does something like what he's done today can claim to be anything else. All that's left to do is to accept it.

That night Lukas slips into an undisturbed sleep from which he does not awaken for another nine and a half hours. He does not dream.

Chapter Twenty-seven

The phone call is what had made it real.

Not when he'd altered the data, not when he'd sent it. Not even the meeting with his attorney, despite the askance looks and unasked questions. It hadn't become real until he'd placed the phone call.

Despite his aversion to using the phone, Lukas had opted to go that route rather than showing up in person so he could avoid the dumfounded expression that would surely splatter across Gladys's face. It had been her idea—she'd mentioned it during the grueling Thanksgiving dinner, yet he had vehemently refused to go along with it, initially. Lukas knew she'd be suspicious, want to know why he had changed his mind. She's old, but not a lot gets past her.

But now, as Gladys sits in the passenger seat of Lukas's Volvo, she appears to have abandoned any suspicions she'd had. She's babbling serenely, interrupting her recollection about the various times she'd been on the university's campus to point out various buildings and blithely explain what businesses used to occupy their premises. Lukas sneaks a quick glance in the rear view mirror. Susan is sitting silently, staring out the back seat window. She's not looking at him.

He's sweating. It's a chilly Friday evening in the first week of December, but as the Volvo proceeds through each intersection and draws closer to Longkesh Music Hall, Lukas's breathing grows a little more shallow. His neck twitches. A slight shiver. The plan is real.

"Susan," Gladys says with glee, pointing out the window, "look at those little wreaths they've got hanging on the lamp posts. Aren't they beautiful?"

Susan gently clears her throat. "Mm, yes, lovely."

Her response sounds forced, Lukas surmises. She doesn't trust this situation. Smarter than she looks.

"Susan, how long since you've visited the campus," Gladys asks.

"Just the once." The significance of the solemn delay that preceded her response is not lost on Lukas.

Gladys continues to talk excitedly, but Lukas ignores her prattling as he eases the Volvo into the parking lot. Pausing to allow a group of well-dressed and heavily bundled visitors to shuffle past, Lukas grips the steering wheel tightly, to downplay the obviousness of his shaking hands and arms. He focuses on tangibles. The flask in his breast coat pocket. Close to his heart. He pulls into a handicapped spot close to the red brick sidewalk, and is out of the car before Gladys and Susan have their seat belts unbuckled.

Despite his mother's protests, Lukas has insisted on using the wheelchair this evening, and he begins wrestling it out of the trunk as Susan emerges from the backseat. She gives him a quizzical look, which he pretends not to notice. The two of them help Gladys into the wheelchair and begin to make their way along the sidewalk beside the vast red courtyard outside the music hall. Lukas pushes the wheelchair as Susan walks alongside, nodding politely at Gladys's nonstop narration. Dusk is gathering quickly. Lukas keeps his gaze focused straight ahead, deliberately avoiding looking high enough to see the familiar bell tower. Lukas notices the birds circling over their heads, but hopes no one else does. Despite the encroaching darkness, they seem unwilling to find a spot to land.

***

Lukas has positioned Gladys's wheelchair in the aisle, and he takes the seat next to her, which puts him in between his mother and Susan, which only adds to his mounting claustrophobia. He looks up. The immense dome seems to stretch halfway to the atmosphere, and they're seated directly underneath it. The epicenter. Lukas loosens his tie, stretches his collar. He thinks of the famous bell that sleeps in iconic silence just above the vaulted ceiling. He finds himself unable to swallow away the rising lump in his throat.

"How do you think they managed to fit it in here?" he hears a voice behind him say. Lukas looks instinctively over at the Christmas tree that towers over the assembling audience like a mountain peak. Right where he knew it would be.

"Luke!"

He jumps at the pressure of Susan's hand on his right arm. She's looking at him, an unreadable expression on her face. She leans toward him slightly, as if expecting a response to something. What does she want? How could she know?

"Your mother asked you a question," she says, with the slow and careful diction of a kindergarten teacher.

He turns. His mother's expression seems clouded with concern. How could they both know?

"Are you feeling alright?" Gladys asks. "You look pale."

Lukas manages a clumsy nod. He fumbles for words. "Fine," he sputters, "I'm fine." He will be soon, anyway. Finally.

There's still time to stop this.

Lukas clenches his eyes closed, tries to calm his breathing. He curses himself for his cowardice. *This is the best way*, he argues with himself.

Susan leans forward. Pointing at something printed in her program, she gushes, "The 'Hallelujah Chorus,' I love that one!" She's talking to Gladys, right past him, as if he weren't even here. He's not sure he is.

"I'll bet this place brings back a lot of memories for you," Gladys says.

Lukas nods. He reaches to loosen his tie and is surprised to find it already is. He feels weak, faint. "Yeah. I guess it does." Memories of bad things that happened, and a few that are about to.

Lukas nearly jumps off his seat as the house lights dim. Only for an instant, and then they come back up. Gladys and Susan peer at him curiously, or maybe accusingly. Possibly both, perhaps neither. Lukas is unable to tell. A warm voice crackles over the P.A. system, explaining that in a few minutes the tree will be lit, and suggesting everyone find their seats.

Lukas tries to force an intake of air through his impossibly constricted throat. He's confused by his ambivalence. Angry, even. Shouldn't an evil man be at ease with committing heinous acts? He places a quivering hand against the flask that lies against his thumping chest. His desiccated mouth longs for a reassuring sip, but he's unable to muster the strength to walk and find a bathroom where he can procure one. Trapped.

The room around him is an indistinct swirl of motion as people move up and down the aisles, in and out of rows, and gradually come to rest in their seats.

There's still time to stop this.

Lukas's eyes draw themselves to the immense crimson curtain that covers the stage. It seems to hang there in timeless omniscience, judgmental in its silent observance. Lukas must close his eyes to avoid its accusing glare. He's seen both sides of that curtain, and it can see both sides of him.

This, he reminds himself, this is what needs to stop. This is not really living; it's not really life, so there's no crime in putting an end to it. It's the best thing for him, and for his mother. And Susan …well, she's shared a part in at least one of his crimes. It will all be over soon. This is the best way.

And the others? Collateral damage, he reasons. You can't save everybody.

"Is that girl who lives at your place in tonight's show?" Gladys says, studying her program.

Lukas's eyes snap open. The possibility had never occurred to him. His whole body shakes; he's certain everyone can see that, but he's powerless to stop it. "No," he mumbles, staring straight at the crimson curtain. "I don't think so." Surely not. She couldn't be. Although he hadn't talked to her lately, about whether or not she was sticking with her music. Hadn't talked to her about much of anything. But, she couldn't be.

"What's her name?"

Lukas can't see the towering curtain that looms in front of him. All he can see is her lonesome dimple. "Katie," he whispers. She couldn't be.

"Reiker?"

The word echoes. His mother's voice seems to be coming from a tunnel somewhere far away. He turns his head toward her, as if in slow motion, and sees her pointing to a name printed in her program.

Somewhere — is it coming from outside? — a dog is barking frantically.

Chapter Twenty-eight

Lukas can't hear a thing.

He had not been able to respond when his mother had indicated the name printed in her program, certain he was hallucinating again. He turns his head slowly, lets his eyes fall upon the program lying in his own lap. His ears feel numbed to all sound waves. He shudders, remembering the last time this happened. He had been backstage, terrified that he was going deaf. Nausea gruffly begins to churn his stomach. With trembling fingers Lukas manages to force open his program. He's certain her name won't be there. It had merely been his morbid imagination.

It's there.

"Carol of the Bells" performed by Katherine Reiker.

His heart double-thumps so violently against his chest that it makes him cough.

You can't save everybody.

"Luke?"

Lukas is unsure how he's able to hear his mother's voice and nothing else. He lets his program fall to the floor. His head turns unsteadily to the left.

"Are you alright, son?"

The shriveled old woman in the wheelchair isn't there.

"What's wrong," she asks. Her shoulder length black hair is pulled back from her face and held in place with plastic clips. Her eyebrows are drawn up, accenting the look of concern in her vibrant blue eyes. This is the woman who would come into his bedroom at night when he was wracked with one of his coughing fits, wrap him in a blanket, and carry him out to the sofa in the living room, where she'd rock him gently on her lap, humming to him quietly until he'd fall asleep. This is the woman who had told him that everything would be alright. And he'd believed it.

No.

Lukas stands. His knees almost buckle, so he grabs the back of the seat in front of him to steady himself. Gladys and Susan look up at him with frank bewilderment. So do several other audience members seated nearby.

"We're leaving," Lukas mumbles. He had intended to say it forcefully, with authority, but it came out sounding more like a question.

"What's gotten into you?" Gladys demands.

He doesn't answer. He steps past her into the aisle and grabs the handles of the wheelchair, yanks it around in an awkward half-circle.

Susan shoots to her feet. "*Lukas*," she hisses.

He ignores her. He ignores his mother's protests as he labors to push the chair up the slight incline of the aisle toward the exits. He ignores the curious and prying looks from the other members of the audience as he passes them. The angle of the aisle is only a gentle slope, but it feels like he's pushing a wheelbarrow full of cement up the side of a mountain. When they reach the spot where the floor levels out at the back of the auditorium, he pauses for just a moment to try to catch his breath. The house lights dim, and a hush falls over the murmuring crowd.

Susan grabs his left arm. Hard. "What's wrong with you?" she charges, nearly out of breath herself.

Lukas won't hear her. Nor will he acknowledge the stream of agitated questions and complaints being emitted by his mother, who's attempting to climb out of the wheelchair. Sounds and demands bounce off his ears, minor dents in the armor of his oblivion. He squints in the weak light, his eyes scanning along the back wall, to the right of the exit doors where the befuddled trio has stopped.

You can't save everybody.

Lukas spots the square red form of the fire alarm several feet away.

"But it can't hurt to try," he mutters aloud. He rushes over to the alarm and pulls it.

Gladys swoons back into the wheelchair. A look of pure fear has replaced the expression of annoyance on her face. Lukas kicks open the exit door and wheels her through it. Susan follows. Before they reach the end of the sidewalk, Lukas hears the door open again. More people emerge from the building, clamoring in confusion. Lukas doesn't stop. He heads away from the building into the open space of the courtyard. He's gasping for breath. Gladys holds onto both arms of the wheelchair as Lukas forces it across the jarring brick surface of the courtyard. Susan struggles to keep up in her high heels.

When they reach the center of the courtyard, Lukas stops. He leans heavily on the wheelchair's handles, heaving and panting. As Susan catches up to them, he looks around her at the crowd that's assembling outside the building. People huddle in groups, shrugging and pointing. Some are putting their coats back on; others are clenching their shoulders for warmth.

Lukas is fairly certain he will vomit. He turns away from the wheelchair, waits for it. The dog's barking intensifies.

Susan is huffing with anger. "What in God's name …" Lukas casts a quick glance at his mother. She's scrutinizing him in silence, clearly terrified.

Susan never finishes her question. She looks at the ground, once she realizes it's shaking. She looks back at Lukas. When the rumbling sound grows loud enough for her to hear it, panic creeps into her eyes. Her purse drops and thuds against the red bricks.

The buzzing of the crowd grows louder as they start to realize what's happening. They begin to migrate away from the building, slowly at first, then faster once the first window shatters.

Lukas clutches the wheelchair handles to keep from falling over, and Susan grabs hold of him.

More people pour out of the music hall, scattering in chaotic confusion. Falling down, tripping over one another. More windows shatter, eliciting screams each time from the panicked crowd. Car alarms add their beeps and whirs to the mounting peal.

Gladys and Susan watch the deranged exodus from the building in a mute state of horror. Scores of people have managed to get a safe distance away and now stand or lean nearby, watching the surreal scene with similar expressions on their faces. Lukas keeps his eyes glued to the bell atop the tower. It begins to sway.

The only other buildings in view are dormitories, which are mostly vacant at this time on a Friday evening, but a few individuals are sporadically emerging from them, their eyes wide and their faces pale. Some are curious to witness the unfolding spectacle; some don't know what else to do.

Lukas is distracted by the wobbling of a slender, twenty-foot birch tree in the parking lot to his left, which pitches backwards and snaps in two when it lands across the hood of a Mercedes. When he looks back up at the bell, its support has begun to give way, and it leans precariously to the left. The volume of the rumbling from the ground has overpowered the sounds of the barking dogs, blaring car alarms, and panicking people. But when the bell breaks free and crashes through the top of the dome, everyone can hear it. They stop and watch. Some scream. Some bring hands to cover their mouths. Everyone grows silent as they hear it smash to the floor of the building in which they had been sitting just moments ago.

Part of the dome has collapsed with the bell, but once each beam in the building has come to rest, either in its place or after having succumbed to gravity, there is an eerie stillness. The rumbling sound has dissipated. The earthquake is over.

The scattered groups of sitting and standing people remain where they are, as if unwilling to allow themselves to believe it's over. Lukas pries his right hand free from the wheelchair and with an unsteady hand withdraws the flask from his pocket. He only spills a couple of drops onto his tie as his quivering hand brings the flask to his lips. Dogs continue to bark. A baby is wailing. Lukas guzzles his drink. Susan watches him in taciturn pause, as if awaiting permission to breathe again.

Slowly, the other onlookers begin to awaken from their comas. They move to find their loved ones. Conversations begin again. A man in a yellow sweater helps two nearby strangers to their feet. A woman takes her cell phone from her purse but only stares at it, as if she doesn't know whom to call.

"Is it over?" Susan whispers.

Lukas nods as he screws the cap back on his flask. He begins to place it back in his blazer's breast pocket, but he stops. Stuffing it in the back pocket of his pants instead, he takes off the blazer and looks around, his gaze in a slow and careful search. He sees her before his eyes spot her.

There, about ten paces away, to the right of Gladys's wheelchair, Katie stands beside a crooked tree. She's looking directly at Lukas, standing with her arms folded across her chest, grasping her shoulders tightly. She's wearing a shimmering, silver satin blouse and a long black skirt, but no coat.

Lukas steps over to her tentatively, looking at the ground.

"You came," is all she says. The tone of the words seems questioning, surprised, and accusatory, all at once. Confusing Katie.

He can't think of what to say, doesn't know the answer to the question in her eyes. It's not a good day for talking. He says nothing. Instead, Lukas holds out his blazer for her, and she takes it.

He turns and walks back to his mother and Susan. "Let's go," he says.

None of them says a word during the ride home.

Chapter Twenty-nine

Lukas stretches the plastic sheeting as tight as he can, staples it into place. He likes the authoritative *shtock* sound of the staple gun. It might not be good for the old window frame, or the blueberry wallpaper, but the sound is empowering.

From her bed behind him, Lukas's mother rattles her newspaper, holding it closer as she squints at it from behind thick glasses. "Three reported dead so far," she mentions. "Lots more injured." She shakes her head, tsk-tsk-ing the article's dreary information.

Lukas lets his eyes close. Three dead. It'll be a long, ugly process when they get to him on judgment day. He forces the numbers out of his head. "It's already about ninety degrees in here, Gladys," he grumbles, stepping back to look at the plastic he's just hung.

She looks at him over the newspaper. "I'm telling you, there's a draft comes through there. Do you want me to catch pneumonia and die?"

"Makes the windows hard to see out of," he says quickly, not allowing himself to ponder her question.

She turns back to her article. "Good thing we were with you last night. You seemed to know what was happening before anybody else."

She's fishing now. Lukas won't take the bait. He focuses on tangibles. Spread. Stretch. Staple.

"What was it that tipped you off?" she continues. "Did one of those fancy machines in your office tell you it might happen?"

Lukas swallows hard, won't turn to face her. It feels hotter than ninety degrees in this room. Careful how you answer, Lukas. "There was nothing in the reports."

Gladys lays the newspaper down on the quilt that covers her lap. She eases off her glasses and rubs her temples. "I can't even read with this headache," she says.

Lukas turns to face her. She looks frail. The young woman with the black hair and the infectious smile—the one in so many of the photographs decorating the room—is no longer recognizable in the wrinkled features and thinning white hair. Lukas wishes he could find her a better pillow, a warmer quilt. He feels a lump lodge itself in his throat. He needs some whiskey to wash the discomfort away.

"Would you do an old lady a favor," Gladys asks.

Lukas's heart double beats.

"Grab a couple of aspirin from my medicine cabinet?"

Lukas smiles. Then again, he thinks as he lays the staple gun on the chair with the inadequate padding in the corner, she'll probably live for another decade. He turns and heads for the adjoining bathroom.

"Above the sink?" he calls out, looking for a moment at his reflection in the mirror, then looking away.

"Yes."

Lukas hears the newspaper rattle. He hopes she's turning to the entertainment section. Horoscope, anything. Opening the cabinet, he surveys the labels of a myriad of prescription and over-the-counter bottles of various shapes and sizes. Together they look like a miniature city skyline, a horizon of pain relief.

"Oh my," he hears his mother's voice call out. "Two stores in a strip mall over on DeValera got completely destroyed. The roofs collapsed." Another tsk-tsk. "That's over near your place, right?"

Lukas grabs the bottle of aspirin and shakes two out into his unsteady hand. "What stores?"

She pauses for a moment, and Lukas finds himself holding his breath. "Uh, a CVS pharmacy," she reads, "and Chadwick's Liquor Store."

Lukas sighs. It figures. Nothing good happens when the earth quakes. He replaces the medicine in its spot and stops, his eyes falling upon a tall bottle of prescription sleeping pills. He picks it up cautiously and reads the label. Turning it in his hand and giving it a light shake, he twitches his lip. At least three-quarters full. He stands in contemplation for a moment. Trying not to rattle the pills inside the bottle, he slides it into his pocket. He hears his mother cough, the newspaper crinkling. He shakes his head. He places the sleeping pills back in the cabinet and hurries out of the room.

Gladys smiles as she accepts the aspirin. He hands her a nearby glass of water and watches her swallow the pills. He replaces the glass for her, then walks over and snatches up the staple gun, turning to scrutinize his work. He listens to the hum of the portable vaporizer behind him.

Gladys watches him for a while, then turns her attention back to the newspaper. "It says there was a much worse one than this back in 1811," she says. "They say the river flowed backwards. Of course, I don't remember very well. I was pretty young back then." She looks up at Lukas, grinning.

Lukas motions toward the ragged edges around the window frames where he's cut the plastic. "You want me to get a blade and trim those up neater?"

She squints, inspecting them. "Nah, it's just fine the way it is." She smiles at him. "Thanks for doing it, even though you think it's silly."

Lukas looks back at the plastic. After a lengthy deliberation, he says, "I'll come back and trim them up tomorrow."

On the way out of the house he sees Susan seated at the dining room table, books and papers spread out before her. He stops and flips through a disheveled pile of mail on the kitchen table.

"Did you get her room all 'winterized'?" Susan calls over to him.

Lukas wags his head. "It's like the Middle East in there," he says, not taking his eyes off the mail he's sorting.

Susan clears her throat. "Hey," she says as though offering a cheerful reminder, "at least Mom got to *see* the campus again."

Mom. Lukas holds up the mail and shoots Susan a quick glance. "No bills I should know about?"

Susan shakes her head. "Everything seems to be okay at the moment."

Lukas nods, drops the mail neatly back onto the table. He turns and heads for the front door.

"You knew it was coming."

Lukas stops in mid-step. He turns halfway around, not fully facing her.

"The earthquake," Susan clarifies, softer. "Didn't you?"

Lukas can feel his face blush. He shrugs.

"Somehow you know these things."

"Not really," he grumbles. Some things are better left unexplained. He gives another half-hearted shrug and says, "I don't know." He longs for a Scotch or two. Or eight.

Susan waits for a lengthy moment before she speaks again. "Can you …" she begins. Her face softens. A tender smile appears. "Will you be coming by tomorrow?"

Surprised, Lukas looks over at her. Her smile is disarming. He considers her question, but realizes he already knows the answer. "Of course I will."

***

The first sound Lukas hears upon entering his house is the crisp clacking of Katie's shoes as she descends the staircase. She's got on a coat and scarf, with her bag slung across her shoulder. Sheepishly closing the door behind him, he watches her feet as they make their way to the bottom of the stairs, not quite able to look her in the eye.

Reaching the alcove floor, she stops in front of him. "Hi," she says softly.

Lukas nods, wondering whether it would be rude to continue moving toward the liquor cabinet as he talks with her.

"Some crazy night, huh?" she says.

Lukas nods again, trying to force a friendly smile. He stuffs his hands in his pockets. "You, ahm … you doing okay?"

Katie dips her head 'yes,' pressing her lower lip tightly against the upper one. The expression dapples her chin with an irregular pattern of tiny dimples, making her look like a child. Sweet Katie. "I'm fine," she says. "Thanks for lending me your jacket. I put it on your bed."

"Okay." It occurs to Lukas that perhaps she's on her way out somewhere, and he's blocking her exit. He takes a couple of steps to his right and leans against the doorway to the parlor.

She's holding the strap of her bag with both hands. She looks slightly away from his eyes. "I was surprised to see you there."

Lukas swallows. "You were?"

She looks back at him. "Yeah, I was," she says, her mouth spreading into a lopsided grin.

Lukas is glad he's leaning against the doorframe; he can't feel his legs. He can't think of what to say, so he continues to nod mutely.

Katie lets go of her bag's strap and crosses her hands in front of her. Letting her gaze drop to the floor in front of Lukas, she caresses the bracelet on her left wrist. Lukas's failure to hold up his end of the conversation is making her uncomfortable, he realizes, and he's angry with himself for it. He remembers when it seemed so easy to converse with her, just a mere hundred or so years ago.

"They think they're gonna be able to save the bell tower," Katie says.

"Yeah?" Lukas purses his lips, his head bobbing in slow acknowledgment. "That's good. It's been there a long time."

"Yeah."

Lukas sneaks a quick glance in the direction of the liquor cabinet. He's tired of this conversation, which consists entirely of the wrong words. He's frustrated that he can't locate the right ones. He tries to think of a graceful way to start wrapping the conversation up, to get Katie going to wherever she's headed and get himself closer to where he needs to be.

"I decided to audition for the Senior Showcase."

Lukas looks up at her, startled somewhat at her abruptness. A smile reaches his lips, and he didn't have to force it. "That's great," he says. "I'm glad to hear that."

She beams, and her dimple makes his smile grow wider. "I'm working on a new piece for the audition, something I wrote." She pats her bag. "That's where I'm headed—to practice it. It's called 'Forgiveness.'"

She looks straight at him, and Lukas can tell the look is supposed to be meaningful, but he's unsure in exactly what way. He ventures a meager guess. "Is it about your mother?"

Katie cocks her head to the side and smiles again, but this one seems to indicate that she's amused by his naiveté, that his guess had been way off. "It's about me," she explains, as if he should have known it all along. Still smiling, Katie walks out the front door.

Lukas stares at the door once it closes. A little more. A little further.

He dashes to the front door, opens it. Standing in the doorway, he sees her stop. She turns to face him, her eyebrows rising expectantly.

Lukas feels his face morphing into magenta. "Your mother," he stammers, forcing the words to come out, "She didn't mean to hurt you." He's fairly certain he won't be able to make her understand, but the look on her face makes him want to try. "She ... well, she didn't mean to make you feel like you weren't ... you know, one of the most important people." He looks down at the cracks in the sidewalk. "I'm sure of it." He closes his eyes, forcing the next words to come out. "You *are*."

Katie's shoulders rise and fall as she draws a deep breath. "In my head, I know my mother didn't mean to hurt me." She drops her eyes, unable to face him. "But she did."

Lukas feels a stabbing pain shoot down through his chest.

Katie continues, "There's no point in pretending it's not there, because it is." She shrugs. "The way I see it, the real point is what I do from here."

"Yeah," Lukas says feebly.

Katie's eyes flicker to his, then back to the ground. "What we both do," she says, almost whispering.

As the sky above them tries on its gray winter outfit, the two stand facing one another, but not looking at each other, as too many moments tick away in silence. Even the cardinal perched on the nearby fence doesn't interrupt.

Finally, Lukas's lips prepare to form words. He's not sure they're the correct ones—that there are any such things—but he forces himself to try. "I'm sure she'd ... change things. If she could."

Katie looks back up at him. "I know what you mean," she says, and it sounds like she truly does. She smiles once more, and this one dissolves the lump in his throat the way a glass of Scotch never could.

Chapter Thirty

It's 2:05 in the rain.

It streaks down like bars across Lukas's office window. He takes the painting down from off his file cabinet, the people dancing under the too-red sky. He wraps it carefully in a large plastic grocery bag to protect it from the rain, and places it on top of the box containing the few other personal items from the office that he's decided to keep. He doesn't need to wait for the meeting on Friday to hear the results of the investigation. Or inquiry, whatever they called it. He knows how it will turn out. Too many people are now in hospitals or graveyards due to a natural disaster they could have been warned about. Possibly. Probably not, but the S.O.C. will be looking for a donkey to pin the tail to. If they find that the data Lukas forwarded to them doesn't match the actual printouts it won't make the decision too difficult.

No sense in putting in a full day's work today.

Lifting the box from his desk, Lukas takes another look around the small office. The needles on the seismograph are patiently scratching the advancing roll of paper, recording their data. Lukas doesn't remember sleeping last night. He doesn't remember arriving at his office this morning, or what he's accomplished in the past four hours, other than packing a small box with mugs, a whiskey bottle, and other useless mementos.

Despite his impending dismissal, his mind has been occupied all day with something else. Lukas can see the smoldering brown eyes as clearly as if she were standing in front of him now. Eyes so eerily familiar that he might have known her all his life, not just for the past four months. The pain behind the eyes that he'd swallow if he could. After she'd walked away yesterday, he had stood in the doorway long after her little green Volkswagen had disappeared around the corner. Then he had finished two-thirds of a bottle of Scotch alone in the parlor. He had thought he'd been drinking for the usual reasons, but at some point late in the evening it had occurred to him that perhaps he was celebrating.

Lukas locks the dismal office and carries the box across the street to his parked Volvo. It's not particularly cold, especially for December, but Lukas is shivering, and the rain makes it worse. A sinister sky overlooks the town, looming a foreboding shade of gray, the color of something dying.

Starting up the engine, Lukas tries to think of a destination to head for, but he can't. So he just drives. He noses the car along streets that are empty, because nobody goes out in the rain. Fog is moving in, hanging low and dense. Even the mountain can't see him today.

Lukas's tires are uneven. They revolve and splash irregularly across the asphalt, producing a peculiar hissing rhythm. The worn out windshield wipers respond with their own squeaky, unorthodox beat. From somewhere under the hood, or perhaps from within the trunk, something floats up like incense, accompanying the rhythm in Lukas's ears.

He catches his breath; his eyes narrow. Quiet at first, delicate, but it's there. A melody. A simple, cascading melody, flowing in rhythm to the tires and the wipers. Lukas is shocked. He has not heard a tune in his head like this for twenty years.

After hearing about Stephen's death, Lukas had walked home through the rain from Longkesh Music Hall, not knowing and not caring whether or not the Senior Showcase was underway. He had not spoken a word aloud for the next eleven days. Then, the twelfth day, it had rained again. Sometime during the night Lukas had pushed his prized hi-fi system out the window of his rented room, sending it plummeting to a violent end in the soggy grass of the back yard. Then he'd called his mother, told her that after finals, he was coming home.

Lukas had never again sat behind a piano.

His enviable record collection, those shiny vinyl disks that had been as important to Lukas as the very air that he breathed, were abandoned. Boxed up and left to collect dust. Basie, Ellington, Monk, Powell. All the talent in the world had been forgotten, set aside on an empty shelf. Including that of Lukas Willow.

The song captivates Lukas. It's definitely not one he's heard before; it's just creating itself—the way they so often used to when he'd be riding in the car during a rainfall, before everything went wrong. It feels like seeing a runaway dog—your best friend you were sure had been dead—wander back up the driveway. Lukas is filled with an incredible sense of lightness; he grips the steering wheel for fear that he might float off the seat if he doesn't. He feels the familiar lump in his throat, but this time he doesn't want to wash it away.

He doesn't stop at the stop sign, not wanting to disrupt the rhythm. He merges right onto the highway, fascinated to see where the magical melody is headed. As his Volvo climbs a slight grade, approaching an old bridge, he wishes Katie were with him. She too would hear the song, he is sure. He can see her beautiful lopsided smile reflected in the rearview mirror. He's gaining speed, and the song grows preoccupied with itself. As the bridge appears in front of him, Lukas notices his thumbs strumming yet another beat quietly on the steering wheel, a full-blown symphony in the rain.

Suddenly the tires skid.

The surface of the bridge is metal, much slicker than the road, and Lukas's grip on the steering the wheel tightens again. Lukas taps the brakes, but the Volvo fishtails, sliding sideways into the other lane. Everything seems to stop moving, and Lukas becomes aware of where he is.

This isn't just any bridge.

It's a route he usually goes out of his way to avoid. His heart sinks. He knows what's coming, knows it's what he deserves. Desperately Lukas steers into the skid. He sees the guardrail coming closer from the corner of his eye. The worn tires, screeching hideously, continue to slide. Lukas closes his eyes. He doesn't need to watch. He's seen it before.

Then, miraculously, the tires catch traction. Control returns, and Lukas coaxes the car to a stop. He blinks, repeatedly, not sure that what he thinks happened actually has. His heart is racing, and his knuckles are white on the steering wheel. The wipers squeak their uneven rhythm. Whirrer-wah, Whirrer, wah. Whirrer-wah.

He has spun completely around and is now facing the other direction on the bridge. That suits him just fine. He draws a deep breath and heads back cautiously in the direction from which he came, refusing to look at the guardrail on his left. The bridge is a series of crude seams between metal plates, which dictate a steady, omnipotent beat against the beleaguered tires. The song is over. The darkness returns.

When Lukas pulls into his driveway, he is still unsure exactly what made him leave the office. He tries to remember the tune, but he can't. He shifts into park, turns off the engine. He doesn't particularly want to go into the house; he's not sure where he wants to be. Leaving the box on the passenger seat, he steps out of the car and into the rain, which is now little more than an aggravated mist. The air seems warmer, and for a moment Lukas fancies taking the long stroll over to campus, to see if maybe he'd run into Katie, offer to listen to her play. Maybe she'd say yes. He dismisses the foolish idea with a swift shake of his head. A good stiff drink sounds like a better idea. It'll help him figure out where he wants to go, what he wishes to be doing. At the very least it will help make his restlessness more tolerable.

Lukas walks toward the dark house with his hands in his pockets. He stops at the foot of the concrete steps.

The itch.

Something is definitely wrong. He closes his eyes, concentrating. His shoulders slump, and he waits. His gray jacket is steadily, evenly darkening in the misting rain. He opens his eyes, stares hard at the front door. Within seconds, he can hear the muffled ringing of the telephone inside. Lukas shakes his head; he should have known it would happen in the rain. Nothing good happens in the rain.

As Lukas turns, Katie's Volkswagen pulls up to the curb.

Well, almost nothing.

She hops out and starts dashing for the front door, daintily holding a notebook flat over her head. The expression on Lukas's face freezes her mid-stride.

"What's wrong," she asks.

"I've got to go to the hospital," Lukas says. "It's my mother."

Katie's perfect forehead wrinkles. She tucks the notebook under her arm and withdraws car keys from her jacket pocket. Without speaking, she turns toward her car and reaches her hand out for Lukas.

And he takes hold of it. Because there are some places you just can't go alone.

About the Author

JEFF GEPHART grew up in a small town outside of Pittsburgh, Pennsylvania, and currently lives in Sacramento, California. He has worked professionally as a graphic artist and as an elementary school teacher. Having written two feature length screenplays and a few short films, Jeff has spent time in front of and behind the camera in a variety of independent film projects and a weekly cable TV show. He also enjoys writing poetry and short stories. *Out of Dark Places* is his second novel.

ALL THINGS THAT MATTER PRESS ™

FOR MORE INFORMATION ON TITLES AVAILABLE FROM
ALL THINGS THAT MATTER PRESS, GO TO
http://allthingsthatmatterpress.com
or contact us at
allthingsthatmatterpress@gmail.com

Made in the USA
Charleston, SC
23 August 2012